What a Gorgeous Day!

You throw on a sweatshirt and walk outside. The waves are breaking against the shore and the air is crisp.

"Good morning!" says Mark, joining you. "It's supposed to be seventy-seven degrees today. You up for a beach day?"

"Sounds good," you say.

"No way," says Bob, walking up. "She's coming horseback riding with me."

"She wants to sit on the beach," says Mark.

"She'll do that tomorrow," says Bob. "She'd rather ride today."

You are sick and tired of being told what you want to do and you are about to tell both of them off when Bruce marches up.

"Anyone want to go to Ensenada with me?" he asks.

Escape, you think, amused by the idea of leaving Bob and Mark to argue with each other.

If you go to Ensenada with Bruce, turn to page 11.

If you try to settle with Bob and Mark, turn to page 95.

FOLLOW YOUR HEART ROMANCES for you to enjoy

Available from ARCHWAY paperbacks

FOLLOW
YOUR
HEART
#10

SEVEN-BOY VACATION

JAN GELMAN

AN ARCHWAY PAPERBACK
Published by POCKET BOOKS • NEW YORK

This novel is a work of fiction. Names, characters, places and incidents are either the product of the author's imagination or are used fictitiously. Any resemblance to actual events or locales or persons, living or dead, is entirely coincidental.

AN ARCHWAY PAPERBACK *Original*

An Archway Paperback published by
POCKET BOOKS, a division of Simon & Schuster, Inc.
1230 Avenue of the Americas, New York, N.Y. 10020

ISBN: 0-671-60299-3

First Archway Paperback printing February, 1986

10 9 8 7 6 5 4 3 2

Printed in the U.S.A.

IL 5+

Read This First!

Seven-Boy Vacation is not an ordinary romance book. It will not make sense if you try to read the pages consecutively. Instead, read until you come to a choice. Then follow your choice to the page indicated. Again, read until you come to a choice; then follow the instructions.

When you reach an ending, the book is not over. Just go back to the beginning and make different choices. You can lose—but only temporarily. There is always another chance.

So follow your heart, read your way to romance, and have a good time.

You read the last paragraph for the tenth time:

You can't say no. You just can't! I promise you'll love it in Los Angeles. You wouldn't believe all the gorgeous guys. And there's so much to do! We can work on the float for the Rose Bowl with the whole volleyball team (guys, of course!). And I'll have my mom's car and we can go anywhere we want. Oh, please, please, please! How can you say no? I miss you! Call me as soon as you get this letter.

Love ya,
Maria

You are so frustrated! When Maria moved to Los Angeles, your mother promised you could go visit her. But the timing stinks.

Last week the Gordons, your parents' best friends, hired you and your friend Karen to apart-

(continued on page 2)

ment-sit while they are in Tahiti. Three weeks of Christmas vacation, completely on your own in a fabulous apartment in the most glamorous neighborhood in New York. You and Karen have been on the phone constantly, making plans and talking about how great it will be to be away from your parents . . . just the two of you. Even though both of your parents will be across town, there will be no nagging, no lectures, nobody to tell you where to go or when to come home!

Maria! you scream to yourself. *How can you do this to me? Why didn't you invite me for the summer . . . or for spring vacation? The two most exciting things that have ever happened to me and I have to choose between them.*

If you decide to go to L.A., turn to page 3.

If you decide to stay in New York, turn to page 7.

"We will be arriving in Los Angeles in ten minutes. The temperature is seventy-four degrees. Thank you for flying . . ."

You hear no more. Your mind stops at seventy-four degrees. You are wearing jeans and a thick sweater; your heavy wool coat is on your lap. It was ten degrees in New York when you left.

You can hardly sit still, and you are the first one out in the aisle when the FASTEN SEAT BELT sign turns off. You rush out of the plane.

There are dozens of people standing around greeting the passengers. Everyone is wearing shorts, miniskirts, summer clothes. And everyone is blond. You look for a girl with long brown hair.

Where could Maria be? you think as the area begins to clear.

A blond girl walks across the room. "Yoo-hoo," she calls in a high-pitched voice. "Do you know where I could find the little girls' room?"

You turn around to face her. "No, I'm sorry," you say. Then you suddenly burst into laughter. "Maria, what are you doing?"

The girl takes off a wig and lets down a long head of dark brown hair. "Well, you know," she says, giggling, "everyone in California is blond."

"You're crazy!" you say, and you hug her. "How are you?"

"Great! Super! And all that. Come on, there's so much to tell you. How was the flight? Any cute boys?"

(continued on page 4)

"Is that all you think about?" you say. "Actually, there *were* two cute guys, typical California blonds. But they sat in the back and I was in the front."

"Oh, is that all you think about?" she says. "Listen to you!"

You pick up your baggage and head to the car.

"What are you doing in those clothes? Did you think you were going to the North Pole?" Maria says. She is wearing a pair of red Bermuda shorts with a white shirt and tennis shoes.

"Hey, don't give me a hard time," you say.

"Oh, but it's so much fun," Maria says as you reach her car. "Listen, I'll drive us home by the scenic beach route."

"The beach!" you shout. "I want to go to the beach!"

"In due time, my dear. In due time. So what's new with you that I don't know about?"

"Oh, not too much. You know just about everything. Oh, yeah, did I tell you that I got contact lenses?" you say.

"You're kidding! So now you can see!" She laughs. "Do you remember the time Mrs. Johnson asked you to read the passage on the board out loud and you had forgotten your glasses? I had to whisper the whole thing to you from behind."

"I wish you still lived in New York," you say.

"I wish you lived here! The things we could do! Just wait till you meet the guys on the volleyball team. You are going to die. I've been the official

(continued on page 5)

scorekeeper at all their games and I'm kind of like family. Just me and twenty gorgeous, crazy guys. It's great!"

"Who's the one you're in love with?" you say.

"Pete. He's terrific. You'll meet him tomorrow. Remember I told you about the Rose Bowl floats? Well, we're working on them tomorrow . . . with the whole volleyball team."

"Look!" you shout. "It's the Pacific Ocean! I can't believe it!"

Directly ahead of you is a bright blue sea, glistening in the sun.

"Let's go down there!" you shout.

"Don't worry, we will!" she says. "But not today. This is just the scenic route to give you a preview of some of the things we'll be doing. This is Venice Beach."

"Okay, okay," you say, staring at four tan, muscular men in tiny little shorts who roller-skate by. "Look at them!"

Maria laughs. "There are better ones. Just wait!"

She turns away from the beach and drives back to the city streets. "We have to stop by Mr. Bryant's restaurant. He's the volleyball coach and part owner of a restaurant. I told him I would let him know if we were taking the team bus to the floats or driving ourselves. I'll let you decide."

She pulls over and parks.

"The bus sounds like fun," you say.

"Well, picture twenty guys in one bus all trying to

(continued on page 6)

top one another's crude remarks. And of course, being the only girls on the bus, we will be the main topic of discussion. Sometimes it embarrasses me to death!"

"So what else could we do?" you ask, walking toward the restaurant.

"Get up at six o'clock and take my mom to work. Then we could have her car."

"Six A.M.?" you say with a horrified look.

"That's the problem."

If you choose to go on the bus, turn to page 105.

If you get up and get the car, turn to page 33.

"I'll meet you there in an hour, okay?" you say to Karen. "Remember, it's 10 East Sixty-seventh Street, apartment 6A. Bye."

You hang up the phone and race around the room. First you throw a big suitcase on your bed; then you open your closet and all your drawers. The blue dress, the pink one, the black one. You pile belts and shoes on top of the dresses. And black pants, khaki pants, turquoise. Underpants, bras, slips, pantyhose, socks, sweatpants.

That's enough, you say to yourself. Then you remember that you haven't put in any sweaters or blouses. You pile them in. *You'd think I was moving out forever,* you think as you stare at the overflowing suitcase. Your makeup! You almost forgot that! You race into the bathroom and fill up a plastic bag with every jar, tube, and container in sight.

When you and Karen took the apartment-sitting job, you decided that except for Christmas day, you wouldn't go home at all; you were going to be truly independent, on your own for the first time in your lives.

You sit on your suitcase and struggle to close the clasps. As you attempt to lift the bag, you happen to glance out the window into the bank that is across the street from your apartment. You can see the bank security guard locking the doors and the last few customers being ushered out. It is three o'clock already!

(continued on page 8)

Oh, brother! you think. *I have fifteen minutes to get uptown!*

You throw your coat on, put your guitar strap around one shoulder, and drag your suitcase behind you into the self-service elevator. You limp through the lobby lugging practically everything you own in life.

As you step out the front door, you spot a cab right in front of you, stopped at the red light. You fling open the door and with all your strength lift your suitcase onto the floor and take a seat, slamming the door behind you.

At exactly the same second that you sit down, the opposite door flies open and a tall, sandy-haired boy about your age jumps in. Your doors slam in unison.

"What are you doing?" you snap. "This is my cab!"

"I'm in a hurry! I've got to be somewhere right away," he says.

"Well, so do I!" you say.

"So? Where to?" the cab driver says in an irritated tone of voice. "I can't sit here all day. The light's changed. Where are you going?"

"Sixty-eighth and Madison!" shouts the boy.

"Hey, wait a minute!" you yell. "I was here first."

"Look, lady. I don't care where I go. But I can't sit here forever." The cab starts to move.

You suddenly realize that Sixty-eighth and

(continued on page 9)

Madison is only one block from where you are going.

"I'm going to Sixty-seventh and Madison," you say, annoyed. "Why don't we just share the cab?"

"Fine. Great. I just have to get there, fast," he says.

What an obnoxious guy! you think as the cab heads uptown.

"So what's your hurry?" he says, looking into your eyes.

Just as you are about to answer, he interrupts. "I have a story to cover. There's a blazing fire in an Italian boutique and they're evacuating the entire block. Things happen fast in this city, and if you're not there when they're happening, you might as well not be there at all."

"What do you mean you have a story to cover? Who do you work for?"

"The New York *Star*. Oh, by the way, I'm Richard. Who are you?"

Strange guy, you think as you look at his crooked smile and his sparkling green eyes. *In spite of his abruptness, he is kind of cute,* you decide. You introduce yourself.

As the cab slowly makes its way through the traffic, you and Richard talk about your schools (he is a freshman at NYU; you are a junior at Stuyvesant High). By the time you reach your destination, you feel like old friends.

(continued on page 10)

The cab stops and you fumble through your wallet for money. Suddenly you realize that in your mad dash out of the house, you put the money somewhere, but not in your wallet. You frantically check through your whole purse. Nothing.

"I . . . uh . . . I can't find my money," you say, wishing you could crawl in a hole. "I mean, I know I have it, but I can't find it."

I can't believe this is happening to me, you think. You have never felt so stupid in your life.

"Don't worry about it. I'll pay the whole thing and you can pay me over lunch at Joe's Pizzeria on Fifty-third and Third tomorrow at twelve-thirty?"

As he speaks, you remember that your money is in your back pocket. You look at Richard.

He's a bit frantic, you think. *But very interesting.*

You reach for your money. Then you stop. If you pay your share of the cab, you may never see him again.

If you pay, turn to page 28.

If you agree to pay him at lunch tomorrow, turn to page 13.

"Do you speak Spanish?" Bruce asks you on the drive to Ensenada.

"I just started Spanish One this year," you say. "I've never really spoken it. Do you?"

"Yes," he says. "I've been studying a lot on my own so that I can converse with the people down here."

Bruce tells you about a family he met last year in Ensenada. "There is a ten-year-old boy and a five-year-old girl. The little boy absolutely adores baseball! I promised him that I would bring him a baseball the next time I came down. Do you mind if we stop by?"

"Of course not!" you say. "I would love to meet them."

The two of you wander around Ensenada for about an hour, looking into shops that sell silver and turquoise jewelry, rugs, sweaters, hats, and little gift items. Bruce is filled with stories about the history of the jewelry, the legends of the Indians in the area, tales of the Spanish settlers. You could listen to him forever.

Bruce stops at a food stand and speaks in Spanish to an old woman. "Si, señor," she says, and fixes you each a fish taco. You love the small pieces of fish, fried and wrapped in a soft tortilla with lettuce and a tart white sauce.

After lunch you drive about ten miles past Ensenada before Bruce pulls into a dirt driveway lead-

(continued on page 12)

ing to a small shack. A little boy and girl run to the car.

"Carlos! Rosa!" Bruce says, and he speaks to them in Spanish. Then he hands the boy the baseball. He gives the girl a little doll.

The children jump up and down and hug him. The girl runs over and hugs you. You feel a flush of warmth through your body.

A heavyset woman in an old, faded, and torn dress comes outside screaming something in Spanish. She stops and smiles when she sees Bruce.

The children rush over to show her the gifts. After accepting some tortillas and a delicious sugared dessert from the mother, you and Bruce take the children back outside. Bruce picks up a big stick and hits the baseball down the driveway. Carlos goes wild chasing the ball. The little girl chases it, too, squealing all the way.

While Bruce teaches Carlos how to hit a ball, Rosa sits next to you. You put your arm around her and she snuggles in close.

On the drive back to the trailer, you are filled with a wonderful sense of completeness. You look at Bruce, so young and shy when he is with his brother, so deep and caring when he is by himself. Spontaneously you reach over and take his hand. He smiles and squeezes yours.

The End

"See you tomorrow!" Richard yells as he gallops up the street.

You struggle to the curb with your suitcase and watch him. He moves like an athlete, with long, graceful strides. You stand there admiring him until he disappears; then you walk toward the front door of your building.

The door bursts open. "You're here!" yells Karen, hugging you and grabbing part of the handle of your suitcase.

Karen looks even prettier than usual. Her jet-black, curly hair has a careless, carefree look; and her lanky, slim body seems to move to some secret music.

"We're doing it!" she says. "We're really doing it! Three weeks alone! I can't believe it."

Her excitement is contagious, and you begin to feel an explosion inside you. "Oh, Karen, this is going to be so fabulous!"

"May I help you with that suitcase?" says a male voice.

You look up into a pair of dark brown eyes and a warm, friendly smile. "Well, sure," you say. "We're going to the sixth floor."

"So am I," he says. "And since there are only two apartments on each floor, I can surmise that you are the young women who will be taking care of the Gordons' apartment while they're gone. May I intro-

(continued on page 14)

duce myself? I'm Craig Radlow. It is my pleasure to welcome you to Ten East Sixty-seventh."

Craig talks as if he were twice your age, but he can't be much more than eighteen. He is wearing a brown crewneck sweater and khaki pants; his impeccably-cut brown hair labels him classic preppie. He takes your suitcase in one hand and Karen's in the other.

"It feels as though you're moving in forever," he says, smiling at you. When you reach the elevator, he motions for you and Karen to get in first. Then he says to the elevator man, "We're all going to six, Jeffrey."

On the way up, you and Karen introduce yourselves to Craig and Jeffrey.

"Well, I'll be seeing you around," says Craig as he drops your suitcases in front of your door. "If you need anything, please ring my bell."

"Thanks," you say. "I'm sure we'll be fine."

You take out your keys and open the door. Two barking, bouncing dogs are suddenly all over you.

"Did you forget to tell me something?" says Karen.

"You mean I never mentioned the dogs?" you say.

"Luckily I love animals," says Karen, petting and playing with the fluffy white Maltese and the copper cocker spaniel.

"Karen!" you scream. "We are free! Free to do what we want! Free to come and go! Free to be messy!"

(continued on page 15)

"This place is like a mansion!" Karen yells from the next room. "I may never leave the apartment. I'll just live in a different room each day."

"Oh, speaking about leaving the apartment," you say. "I had the weirdest cab ride up here." You tell Karen about Richard. As you are telling her, you suddenly get very nervous about meeting him tomorrow. You don't even know him. Suppose he doesn't show up? Or worse, suppose he shows up and you can't think of anything to say to him? Or suppose he turns out to be a colossal creep?

Maybe I should ask Karen to go with me, you think. *I'd certainly feel more comfortable! But wait a minute,* you tell yourself. *Here I am taking complete charge of an apartment, trying to be a responsible adult, and I'm going to bring a friend as a security blanket?*

Besides, every guy who ever sees Karen falls in love with her. And Richard is really cute and interesting. You sort of would like to save him for yourself.

If you ask Karen to go with you, turn to page 20.

If you meet Richard by yourself, turn to page 37.

You gather up the dogs and rush home.

"What do you wear ice-skating?" you ask Karen as you flip through the pile of sweaters on the floor near your bed.

"How do I know? I've never been skating," says Karen.

"Oh, brother!" you say, holding up a red sweater. "I see disaster and bruises in our future."

"Here, put this one on," says Karen, tossing you a big wool beige sweater. "It's warmer. And put on this turtleneck underneath."

Karen puts on a thick blue sweater, and you are out the door.

"This is crazy!" you say as you ride down in the elevator. "They're going to know that we came to see them!"

"So?" says Karen. "We *did* come to see them."

You arrive at Rockefeller Plaza and walk toward the huge outdoor skating rink, set below street level. You stand at the rail and join the crowds of people staring down at the skaters.

"We're really going to go down there, huh?" you say. "I don't even see them. They aren't here."

"They will be," says Karen, pulling you down the stairs and toward the rental department.

"I can't believe I'm doing this," you say, staring at all the people who are going to watch you make a fool of yourself.

Soon you step onto the ice, clutching the rail.

"Maybe I can just watch from here," you say.

(continued on page 17)

"Come on," says Karen. And she pulls you away from the rail. You both go down in a pile.

"Ouch!" you yell. Karen laughs.

"Uh-oh," she says, looking across the ice. "There they are."

"Where? Where?" you scan the rink. Suddenly your eyes stop. Jon and Greg are standing with two girls.

"Oh, great!" you say. "This is going to be fun." Now you really feel stupid. "Karen, this could possibly turn into the most embarrassing moment of my life."

"You know, I have to agree," says Karen.

You both watch as the boys help two cute blondes onto the ice.

"They haven't seen us yet!" Karen says. "We could go!"

If you try to escape without being seen, turn to page 52.

If you stay, turn to page 61.

"See you in a while," says Maria as she walks out.

"I'm glad you stayed," says Dan, looking into your eyes. His compelling green eyes and long dark lashes seem to draw you into him.

Dan tells you that he is going to NYU to study anthropology. "I've always wanted to learn about different cultures, how different people live."

Your best friend's father, Dr. Jolly, is a physical anthropology professor at NYU. You tell Dan that you will introduce him.

"Fantastic," says Dan. He hugs you. "You're the best thing that ever happened to me! To tell you the truth, I was really scared about going to New York. Now I can't wait!" He takes your hand. "I sure am glad you chose to spend your vacation in Los Angeles."

I am too, you think. *A vacation that's going to follow me home.* You squeeze his hand and look into his smiling eyes.

The End

"I was hoping I'd get to see Dan again," you say.

"Oh, yeah, I forgot. We'll go back now."

You drive to the other party. *I hope he's not mad,* you think.

You turn down the once-crowded street. There are no cars.

You pass the house. There is no noise.

"Looks like it got broken up," says Maria.

"Yeah, I guess so," you say. *He was really special,* you think, furious at yourself for walking out on him.

The End

"So, I get to meet the mystery taxi boy . . ." Karen says as you fiddle with your hair for the tenth time, parting it on the side, middle, and back to the side.

Karen jumps in front of you and begins to hum a romantic love song as she strums an imaginary guitar. "And now we continue with this week's episode of . . . drumroll, please . . . *Life in a Taxicab!*"

You hit her and she laughs.

"As they look piercingly into each other's eyes," Karen continues dramatically, "the handsome boy whispers softly into her ear, 'Will you do me the honor of allowing me to escort you uptown?'" Karen jumps up, arms flung out.

"She smiles sweetly and looks romantically into his emerald-green eyes." She hums again, slowing the tempo.

"'Yes,' she whispers, and the cab drives off into the traffic."

Karen falls on the floor, laughing. You can't help laughing also.

I guess this is pretty ridiculous, you think as you put your coat on.

When you and Karen reach the pizzeria, a sudden nervousness flows through your body. *What if I don't recognize him?* you think. *Thank goodness Karen is with me!*

"Hey, how about a cab ride?" a male voice says behind you. There stands Richard, and you definitely recognize those deep-green eyes.

(continued on page 21)

You introduce Karen and the three of you sit down at a booth.

"So, I saw a great show last night off-Broadway called *The Old Times*," Richard says, breaking the ice.

Before you have a chance to open your mouth, Karen begins. "Oh, I've wanted to see that all year. Tell me all about it. Are you an actor? I'm an actress; well, I hope to be. Unfortunately, I don't get to see as many shows as I should because they're so expensive."

"No, I'm not an actor, but I have a passion for the theater. And I get free tickets for nearly all the shows from the newspaper. Lots of times I get two tickets. Would you like to go with me sometime?"

You know immediately that you are in big trouble. Karen goes to school at Performing Arts, the school that the television show *Fame* was modeled after. She dances, acts, and sings. And she lives, breathes, and drinks theater. You lean back and wait for the pizza to arrive, knowing that there's no way you are going to get a word into this conversation.

Karen and Richard are deeply into discussing an actor you have never even heard of when a beep goes off in Richard's pocket.

"What was that?" you ask.

"Oh, nothing," says Richard, taking a beeper from his pocket and turning it off. "The paper beeps me all the time. I can ignore it if I want to." He turns

(continued on page 22)

to Karen. "So tell me, have you ever auditioned for anything outside of school?"

You feel totally in the way.

When the pizza comes, you dive in, eating twice as much as either of the others.

. . . and they ride happily into the traffic, you think. *Sure! Richard and Karen, that is!*

The End

"Let us out here!" you say.

"Yes, ma'am!" the cab driver says, pulling over.

You pay him and scurry over to the theater, flinging out your guitar and beginning to play. You are playing loud, sharp, spunky tunes, relieving all your anger by playing aggressively. Karen's voice is loud and clear and beautiful.

People once again stop to listen. In only a few minutes you are smiling again.

An older couple stands to the side through four songs. The man is tapping his foot and they are talking animatedly. When you take a break, the man walks over to you.

"Hello, there!" he says in a warm, friendly tone. "My name is Jerry Torenson."

He hands you a business card.

"I am presently producing a movie for Columbia Pictures, and I would love to use you two in one of the scenes. It is a setting similar to this, except we are shooting it outside a theater in London. You both have a lot of talent and I know you'd add character to the scene."

You are speechless. An offer to be in a movie!

"If you are interested, come down to my studio Monday around noon," he adds. "We've got to run. The curtain goes up in two minutes."

"We'll be there!" Karen calls after him.

You stand still for a moment. Then you and Karen look at each other.

(continued on page 24)

"Do you think he's legitimate?" you say. "I mean this city is full of con men. And how about all those stories about young girls being lured into prostitution? What do you think?"

"I've heard of him," says Karen, looking at the card. "But suppose he's impersonating the real Jerry Torenson?"

"I think we have to check him out somehow," you say.

"I know what we can do!" screams Karen. "My uncle does advertising for Columbia Pictures. He could tell us if this guy is real, and if this address is his real office. Oh, my gosh! I can't stand it!"

When you get home, Karen tries to reach her uncle, but there is no answer. You cannot sleep all night.

"You still awake?" you say to Karen at about three in the morning.

"Yeah," she mutters. "First your brother, then the movie. It's all too much."

Finally you doze off.

"Wake up! Wake up!" Karen says, rolling you over. "I just called my uncle and he's calling me back. It's eight-thirty in the morning. If I can't sleep, neither can you!"

You get up and wander for the next half hour.

"He's probably a con man," you say. "It's too good a story to be true."

The phone rings and you both jump.

(continued on page 25)

"Hello," says Karen.

"Yes. Yes. He is! You're sure? I can't believe it! Of course I will. Thank you. Thank you. I love you."

You are jumping up and down.

"Yahoo!" you both scream. "We're going to be in the movies!"

The End

You can hear screams and music as you drive up the crowded street. Cars are parked everywhere for blocks. You squint to see the herds of people standing outside Lesley's house. You are nervous about a party like this, but Maria assures you that you'll have fun.

You park the car a few blocks away and walk toward the house.

"Hey, there, girls!" yells a male voice. There are three guys standing next to a car, but you cannot see what any of them look like.

When you are finally through the gate, you look around for Dan, but you cannot see anyone unless you are very close. The party is packed with kids, all of whom look like a big blur.

"Hey, Maria," a thin blond guy says, "let's dance."

Someone standing next to him asks you to dance. The four of you go out onto the dance floor. As you dance you glance around, looking for Dan. Everyone looks like him.

You are feeling overwhelmed by the oversized, noisy, blurry crowd. You are used to parties where you know everyone . . . parties with no more than twenty-five people. There must be hundreds of kids at this one.

For the rest of the night you follow Maria around. She introduces you to dozens of people. You dance; you talk; you laugh. All of her friends are a lot of fun, but you can't keep your mind off Dan. You look

(continued on page 27)

everywhere, wishing he would find you . . . but it never happens.

On the way out Lesley stops you. "Did you find Dan?" she says. "He was looking for you earlier."

"No," you say, disappointed.

"Well, he told me that he thought he saw you, so he waved. When you didn't wave back, he figured he had the wrong person."

You are crushed. *I never saw anyone waving at me,* you think, furious that you chose not to wear your glasses. *That's much too high a price for vanity,* you think.

The End

"Hey, wait a minute! I just found some money," you say, pulling out a five-dollar bill from your back pocket.

"Okay," he says, taking the money and giving you a dollar back. "I can take a hint. See you around!"

He jumps out the door and runs down the street. You struggle into the building and meet Karen. As you are riding up in the elevator, you suddenly remember something.

"By the way," you say. "I hope you like dogs. We've got two of them."

"Great!" Karen says. "You know I love animals. Any bears? Lions?" Karen throws back her head and roars. Her curly dark-black hair flies like a mane; her dark eyes sparkle.

You open the door to the apartment and a little white Maltese and a cocker spaniel four times its size pounce on you.

Karen laughs as she picks up the Maltese. "You call this a dog?" She giggles, rubbing noses with the tiny animal. "You look like a cotton ball. LBF. That's what I'm going to call you. Little Ball of Fluff."

"Her name is Mercedes," you say.

"Not to me," says Karen, putting the dog down and turning her attention to the cocker spaniel. "What's your name?"

"That's Corky," you say.

"Corky the copper-colored copper spaniel. I mean cocker spaniel. Hey, that's a tongue twister."

(continued on page 29)

Karen dances around the house trying to sing Corky the copper-colored cocker spaniel, but blowing it every time. You join her.

"Corky the copper-colored cockered . . . I mean . . . oh, forget it!" you shout.

"We're all alone. It's just us for three weeks!" screams Karen. "Look at this place. It's beautiful. I didn't know New York had such huge apartments." She runs over to the window. "Look, the park is right here. Doesn't it look gorgeous with last night's snow? Let's go play."

"You sure are hyper," you say. "Let's take the dogs with us."

"Come on, LBF!" Karen says, picking up the Maltese. You search out their leashes and head for the park.

The ground and trees are covered with a blanket of snow. Karen throws a snowball at you. Corky starts barking. You let him off the leash and he bounds into a pile of snow.

"LBF is camouflaged in the snow," Karen says. "Hey, let's build a snowman."

"There's not enough snow for a snowman!" you yell. "How about a snowdog?"

You begin rolling a snowball, adding more and more snow to the lump as you roll. Karen comes over with her ball and you put them together and begin to shape the packed mound into the shape of a dog. You are carefully molding the head when Karen tosses a snowball at you.

(continued on page 30)

"Hey!" you yell, and throw one back. Another returns, hitting you smack in the face.

"That's it!" you yell, laughing. "Come on, Corky. Let's get her!" You chase after Karen, bombarding her with snowballs. Finally you stop and make a giant ball, packing it as hard as you can. You fling it with all your might at Karen, screaming a battle cry as you throw. Karen ducks.

"Hey!" a male voice yells.

Oops! You look over at a medium-height, blond-haired boy with a blue-and-white striped scarf and a pair of skates around his neck. His navy-blue ski sweater is covered with snow.

"Now what did I do to deserve that?" he says.

"Nice shot!" calls his curly-haired friend.

"I'm sorry. I didn't mean it. I was—"

"Hey, no problem. I'll just let my lawyer handle it," he says. "Greg?"

The curly-haired boy walks up to you. His dark hair accentuates his blue eyes. "Name, phone number, favorite food, and shoe size, please," he says.

You laugh.

"Okay, skip the shoe size."

You laugh again.

"Okay, okay. We'll stick to names," he says. "I'm Greg. This is Jon."

You tell him your first names. Just then, Corky comes bounding over with LBF following right behind. He runs right past you and jumps on Jon.

(continued on page 31)

"Cute! Cute dog!" Jon says, wiping snow from his pants. "You two girls are dangerous."

"Corky, come here!" yells Karen. "Leave these nice guys alone."

"She said we're nice!" Greg says. "Did you hear that?" He hits Jon. "Say it again."

You and Karen look at each other and giggle.

"Well, Greg," says Jon. "We'd better go. We still have to pick up your skates and get down to Rockefeller Plaza by five."

"Right," Greg says. "I guess so!"

"Girls," says Jon, turning toward you and Karen, "I hope we run into each other again. And do be careful with the snowballs. I want to feel that I am the only one you've hit today. It is special." He winks at you and walks away.

Karen collapses into the snow. "Have you ever met two pair of blue eyes so gorgeous in your life?" she says, sighing. "How am I going to marry Greg if he leaves me like this?"

"Anyone for ice-skating?" you say, giggling.

"Brilliant idea!" says Karen.

"I was kidding, Karen. Neither of us has ever been on skates. We'd look like total idiots!" you say.

"So?" she says.

If you go ice-skating, turn to page 16.

If you don't, turn to page 65.

"Listen," you say, returning to the table. "Something just came up and I have to run. I'm really sorry."

Then you remember the money. "Oh, I almost forgot!" You reach into your wallet. "Here's the money I owe you. I'm awfully sorry."

You quickly put on your jacket and try to avoid looking at Richard.

"Is there something I can do?" he asks. "Would you like me to come with you?"

"No, no . . . I'll be fine. Thank you."

You rush out the door.

That really showed him, you think. *Now he knows what it feels like.*

You walk along the street looking in the shop windows. You stop for a while to look at some stuffed animals displayed in a forest made of stuffed trees and bushes.

I'm never going to see him again, you think.

You stare into a restaurant window. There is a young couple laughing together at a table near the window. You think of Richard.

Whose loss was this anyway? you wonder as you quickly walk home.

The End

That night you and Maria are up until four in the morning talking. You finally doze off.

The next thing you know, Maria is shaking you. "I don't believe it," she says. "It's ten o'clock!" My mom has already left with the car, and the volleyball bus took off at nine."

You flop down in bed. "Oh, well. *C'est la vie!*"

After eating breakfast you and Maria take a public bus down to Venice Beach, where Maria convinces you to rent roller skates.

You put on your skates and your elbow and knee pads, and you take off down the crowded boardwalk. A woman in a bikini roller-skates past you; a man walks by in a white turban; then another man with a white beard and a woman's long dress waves to you. Two huge muscular men walk past you in little Speedo swimsuits, flexing their muscles.

You stop to join a crowd watching a man juggle a chainsaw, an apple, and a shoe.

"The chainsaw is on!" you say.

"I know," says Maria. "He's nuts."

You skate past outdoor cafés, food stands, and people selling T-shirts, sunglasses, shoes, clothes. You slow down to look at the fortune-tellers, musicians, bikers, joggers. A huge crowd surrounds a bunch of young people break dancing.

"This is amazing!" you say, turning around in circles. You skate on.

CRASH! You bump smack into a small blond girl and both of you land on the ground.

(continued on page 34)

"I'm sorry," you say. "Are you all right?"

"Yeah, I think so," says the girl as Maria skates over.

"Lesley!" Maria says. "What are you doing here?"

"Well," says Lesley, "I thought I was skating."

"I see you've already met my friend from New York," says Maria, introducing you.

"And this is Dan, an old friend of mine," says Lesley, turning to a boy who has been standing near Maria. He is about medium height with sun-streaked brown hair and bright green eyes.

"Pleased to meet you," you say.

"Did I hear that you're from New York?" he says. "Where? I'm going to school at NYU next year."

"I live two blocks from NYU," you say.

"Hey, listen. I've never been to New York and I would love to talk to you about it. I really don't know what to expect," says Dan.

You have been feeling a little like an alien being all day . . . the Venice scene has been incredible, but somewhat disarming. The idea of talking about New York to someone who really wants to hear what you have to say is very appealing.

Lesley interrupts. "I'm having a party tonight. Why don't you guys come?"

"We could talk then," says Dan. There is something about the way he looks at you that makes you feel good. He is totally focused on your eyes . . . and looking at his in return makes you feel strangely

(continued on page 35)

bonded to him. You are pleased when Maria promises to come to the party.

You and Maria spend the rest of the afternoon skating, bumping into people, and laughing. You buy a pair of earrings for a dollar. Before you know it, it is five o'clock. You return your skates and take a bus home.

"I'm really looking forward to seeing Dan again," you say while eating a tuna fish sandwich. "I kind of liked him. What should I wear?"

"I don't know," says Maria. "I don't even know what I'm wearing."

"You live here! What do you wear to a party in California?" you say, rubbing your eyes. "Sometimes I really hate contact lenses. They've been bothering me all day."

You try on a pair of white cotton pants . . . too summery; black pants . . . too tight. Finally you decide on a pair of gray pants. They match Maria's gray-pink-and-white checkered sweater perfectly.

"Put on my pink boots and you'll be set!" she says.

"Pink boots! No way," you say, putting on your white pumps. "This is fine, thanks. Look what California has done to you. Pink boots!"

"I'll be right back," you say, going into the bathroom. Your eyes have been watering and hurting. You look in the mirror at red, irritated eyes.

You remove your contacts and put them into the case. Your eyes still hurt and there is no way you can

(continued on page 36)

put the lenses back in. Your rub your eyes in relief. Then you look around. Everything looks like a big blur. You look into the mirror. *I look like a disaster,* you think, rubbing off smeared mascara from under your eyes.

"Ta-da!" Maria says, jumping next to you in a bright blue jumpsuit. She looks a bit out of focus.

"Oh, baby," you say. "Watch out, guys!" She laughs, swinging her hips.

You squint at the clock across the room. You are so used to your contacts that not being able to see distance is a shock to you. Your dig out your glasses and put them on.

"Gross!" you shout, looking in the mirror. "Dan won't even look at me with these things on!"

"He will, too!" says Maria.

You hate yourself in glasses, but you can't see anything too far away without them.

If you wear the glasses to the party, turn to page 111.

If you don't, turn to page 26.

"Mirrors should be outlawed!" you yell.

You have tried on at least six sweaters, three of yours and three of Karen's. They all look horrible. You finally decide on the first one, a pink-and-blue bulky knit that rests on your hips.

Someone's going to mistake me for a blimp, you think, wishing Karen were there.

Karen has an amazing instinct for fashion; she can always coordinate the perfect outfit for you.

You glance at your watch. Twelve-fifteen. Panic strikes. You have fifteen minutes to meet Richard.

"My keys!" you yell.

Frantically you toss your clothes off the bed, finally digging up your keys at the bottom. You grab your purse and coat and rush out the door. By now it is twelve twenty-five, and you have fourteen blocks to walk, rather, run.

You dodge through the crowds of workers and shoppers, wishing you could blow a whistle and part the people down the middle. When you reach the restaurant, Richard greets you at the door.

"I was beginning to get worried," he says as you follow him to a booth. "I even ordered a pizza. Hope you like pepperoni."

You apologize for being late. "I love pepperoni. Now, if you had ordered anchovies, I'd be in trouble."

"So, tell me about yourself!" Richard says, leaning his chin on his hands and looking at you.

Oh, brother! you think. *What do I say to that?*

(continued on page 38)

"Well," you say, "I grew up in Greenwich Village, and—"

You are suddenly cut off by a beeping sound.

"My beeper!" Richard yells. "I've got to get to a phone. Excuse me, please." He runs off.

You are confused. The only people you know with beepers are doctors.

Richard returns with an anxious look on his face.

"There's a demonstration over by the U.N. that's getting out of control. I've got to get over there for the paper. Look, I'm really sorry . . . can we meet tomorrow? Same time . . . same place. I'm really sorry!"

He throws a ten-dollar bill on the table. "That'll cover the pizza. We can take care of the details tomorrow. See ya." He rushes out the door.

"Hey, wait," you yell, hoping for more of an explanation. But he's gone. Just then, the pizza arrives.

"I'll take it home!" you say, handing the waiter the money. You know that your face is bright red.

All the way home you think about the nerve of Richard. And to make things worse, not only do you owe him the four dollars from the cab, but now you owe him another four dollars from the pizza change. You *have* to meet him tomorrow.

By the time you get home, you have decided that maybe it wasn't such a horrible thing. After all, he does want to see you. Besides, you've never met a newspaper reporter before.

You plop down at the kitchen table, take out a diet

(continued on page 39)

soda, and proceed to eat two slices of lukewarm pizza.

When Karen comes home she convinces you that you shouldn't be angry.

The next day you walk back to the pizzeria in a good mood.

"Hi!" says the man at the counter. "Are you here to meet Richard?"

"Yes," you say, suddenly feeling a knot in your stomach.

"He just called to say that he can't make it. He's really sorry. He hopes you'll be able to meet him tomorrow at one o'clock at the Omelette Parlor on Seventy-third and Lexington."

"Thank you!" you say, certain that steam is coming out of your head.

How could he do that? I have wasted two days on this idiot, and he thinks he can just leave a message for the next place he's not going to show up at. You are fuming.

"No way!" Karen shouts when you tell her. "I don't believe it! Why do guys think they can do things like that?"

"I sure don't know," you say. "I could never do that to someone!"

"That's it!" shouts Karen. "We've got a plan!"

"A plan for what?"

"Sit down, my dear. Here's what we're going to do." She points her finger at you. "You are going to go to the Omelette Parlor tomorrow—"

(continued on page 40)

"Oh, no, I'm not," you interrupt.

"Sit tight," Karen says. "Listen to me. You will go there, sit down, have a short conversation, at which time I will call and ask that you be paged. You will take my call and then return to the table and announce that you have to leave unexpectedly. And you will walk out of the restaurant leaving twinkle toes at the table alone." She nods her head. "Well, what do you think?"

"I like . . . I like . . ." you say.

"Good. Then, it's set!" Karen says.

The next day Karen picks out a pair of tight black jeans, a gray blouse, and a gray and red sweater for you to wear.

"You'll knock him dead!" she says. "That jerk is going to take one look at you and know what he's missing. Listen, wear this bright red scarf so I can describe you to the hostess."

You are a bit uneasy about this whole thing. The idea is great; you just wish someone else were doing it. Besides, a part of you kind of likes Richard, even though he is a flake.

You wander into the kitchen and pour yourself some orange juice. As you are returning the container to the refrigerator, you accidently knock over an open canister of sugar.

The mound of white on the floor reminds you that you don't even know where they keep the vacuum cleaner. Instead of looking, you grab a section of *The New York Times* and sweep the sugar with a

(continued on page 41)

sponge onto the paper. Then, holding the paper carefully, you open the door into the back hallway where the garbage cans are kept.

You have never been in this hallway before. As you are trying to pry open the lid of the can, you suddenly feel a hand on your shoulder. You panic and throw the sugar and paper into the air with a squeal.

A male figure jumps back, away from you. You are so frightened you can barely see.

"It's me!" says a voice. "Your neighbor. I'm sorry I scared you."

You can see now that the strange man who has terrified you is Craig, the boy you met in the elevator when you arrived. He is standing in front of his back door, shaking sugar out of his hair.

Oh, no! you think. *What have I done now?*

"I am so sorry," he says.

"Oh, no," you say. "*I'm* sorry. I certainly overreacted. Look at you." As you brush sugar off his shoulder, you notice that he is wearing a heavy white apron.

"It's okay. Don't worry about it. Cooks enjoy wallowing in food."

"Oh?" you say. "Are you a cook?"

"Ever since I was a kid. My father was the U.S. ambassador to France, and I was introduced to the glories of French cooking when I was seven. By the time I was ten, I was an expert cook. For the last six months I have been catering dinner parties."

(continued on page 42)

"Wow," you say. "I'm impressed! Maybe before I leave you'll cook something for me. Karen and I could buy the ingredients."

"Oh, sure. But I have a better idea. I'm catering a Christmas party for some of my father's business friends, the Newmans, next week; and at this very minute I am preparing some of the dishes as sort of a trial run. I like to test new recipes on friends. My mother and a friend of hers are going to be my guinea pigs. Will you join us? Your friend is welcome, too. We'll be sitting down in about ten minutes."

You know that Karen has plans. And you do, too. But this sounds a lot more interesting than walking out on Richard.

If you accept the invitation to be a guinea pig, turn to page 53.

If you stick to your plans, turn to page 49.

"It's all taken care of," you say. "I'm apartment-sitting with a friend, and one of the dogs is sick."

"Will it be all right?" asks Richard.

"Yes. I forgot to tell my friend that the dog has an allergy. She just has to give him a pill and he'll be fine."

A new lie to cover an old lie, you think. *I hate this! Richard seems genuinely concerned. I'm so glad I didn't walk out on him.*

The waiter comes over and takes your order. For the next half hour, you and Richard talk nonstop. By the time you are halfway through the omelette, it feels as though you are old friends.

"You know," Richard says as he pops the last of his English muffin into his mouth, "I feel as if I've known you forever."

"Me, too," you say. You have never been so comfortable with a boy before. There's something different about Richard, something exciting.

Just then, you hear a beeper. *No, not again,* you think as Richard excuses himself to go to the phone. You nibble on the last bites of your mushroom and cheese omelette.

I can't believe this is happening to me! He's going to leave again! you think. *I should have just walked out when Karen called.*

Richard comes rushing back. "This is it! This is the big one! I'm sorry to do this to you again, but listen to this: a bank robbery in progress with hostages at Ninth and University . . ."

(continued on page 44)

Your heart jumps. "That's where my family lives!" you shout. "We use that bank! My mother could be one of those hostages!"

"Then come on!" He grabs your hand, and you both scramble through your pockets for money.

You drop a ten-dollar bill on the table and rush out the door. Richard hails a cab and you climb in. He laughs.

"Why are you laughing?" you say.

"Look where we are again!" he says. "And not only that, but I met you at Ninth and University. We're returning to the scene of our beginnings."

He reaches over and takes your hand. "It took a lot of perseverance, but I'm glad we're where we are."

"What do you mean by that?" you ask.

He doesn't answer. Instead, he just looks into your eyes and squeezes your hand.

When the cab turns down University from Fourteenth Street, the traffic is backed up, moving inch by inch. You pay the driver and run down University toward Ninth. There is a blockade at Tenth Street, and a police officer is rerouting pedestrians.

"Sorry, kids. You can't go down there," he tells you.

"But I live there!" you say.

"Sorry, there's some trouble. Orders are, no one gets through."

"I'm press," says Richard, pulling out his press pass.

(continued on page 45)

"Sorry. My orders are nobody," says the policeman.

You look at Richard. "Come on!" you say, and you grab his hand and turn down Tenth Street. "This is the back end of my building. It runs the whole block from Ninth to Tenth Street. We can go in the Tenth Street entrance and walk through to Ninth Street. My apartment is on the second floor facing Ninth."

You pull Richard into the Tenth Street side of your building and take the elevator to the basement. Then you walk down the dimly lit corridor, past the storage rooms, past the handyman's workshop to the Ninth Street elevator. You take the elevator to the second floor and ring the bell of your apartment. No one answers, so you open the door with your key and rush to the window in your bedroom, carefully stepping over the piles of clothes and junk on the floor.

"Sorry about the mess," you say.

"Are you kidding?" says Richard, opening the window. "This is fantastic! I can see and hear everything. You didn't tell me you could see the inside of the bank. This is incredible!"

Outside the bank there are police everywhere . . . behind cars, at the sides of doors, on the roof.

"Would you look at that!" Richard yells. "I can see the hostages on the floor in the back."

You rush over and look out, suddenly worried about your parents.

(continued on page 46)

"Binoculars," you say. "My brother's binoculars!" You race into his room, grab them, and run back to the window. Your parents are not among the hostages, but with the binoculars you can see the fear in the eyes of the people lying on the floor.

"This is Sergeant Hoolihan," a loudspeaker announces from below. "We have to see that the hostages are alive!"

"They're alive; I can see them!" says Richard to nobody, scribbling notes on his pad.

"We have to let them know," you say.

The loudspeaker blares again. "We need to see the hostages before we can negotiate."

"Hey, up here!" Richard yells to a police officer just beneath the window. "Come up to the second floor."

"What are you doing, kid? Shut that window! Get inside!"

"No. Come up here. We can see the hostages!" you yell.

In less than a minute there are eight policemen in your room. You kick the clothes under your bed as they file in.

Richard doesn't stop writing and asking questions. "What a story!" he says as he scribbles more.

You watch and listen as the police communicate by walkie-talkie with the men on the ground: "The hostages are being led into the safe. The door is closed. All eight hostages are in there. This is our chance."

(continued on page 47)

Suddenly there is a shot fired from inside the bank. Richard pulls you down. Your heart is pounding. There are more shots, more walkie-talkie, more loudspeaker. The noise, the voices, the shots bombard your ears until it is all a jumble of harsh, unintelligible, seemingly endless sounds.

Finally one of the policemen announces that it's over. Richard questions him for details: One of the robbers has been killed; two of them have been taken to the hospital; a security guard has also been injured. And one of the hostages has suffered a heart attack.

Richard is immediately on the phone, reading his story to someone at the paper. You are amazed at his facility with words; somehow the story was written while the world was in chaos.

You are just ushering out the last policeman when Richard hangs up the phone.

"Are you all right?" he asks.

"Yes. Just a bit shaken up," you say.

He puts his arms around you and holds you tight.

"You know," he says, "you are some kind of girl. I've never met anyone like you before."

You smile. "And *I've* never met anyone like you!"

He puts his hands on your shoulders. "Let's take a walk through SoHo; and afterward, I've got this great little restaurant where we can go for dinner."

"These meals we eat together sure are interesting," you say.

"You're right," he says. "A little too interesting."

(continued on page 48)

He reaches into his pocket, takes out the beeper, and turns it off. Then he leans over and kisses you on the cheek.

"Come on," he says. "Let's go. We have a lot of catching up to do."

The End

You practice as you walk across Seveᴺty-third Street. *I'm awfully sorry, but that was an emergency call. I've got to run. No, sounds dumb. How about, Hey, something came up; gotta go. No, too abrupt. Shoot! I don't know what to say. Maybe he won't even show up.*

You tighten Karen's red scarf around your neck. Suddenly someone taps you on the shoulder.

"Going my way?" a male voice says.

You turn around. It's Richard! You weren't ready for him yet. His warm smile and cheerful voice make you feel guilty.

"Hey, I've never seen this place before," says Richard, stopping in front of a small, cozy French restaurant. "Let's try this instead. I feel like a big spender. Besides, I owe you."

This is not part of the plan, you think. *What about Karen?*

"Uh," you stammer, "that does look good; but I have been craving an omelette all day."

"Okay, no problem. We'll stick to the plans."

Now he probably thinks I've been thinking about him all day. You feel uncomfortable. You always do when you lie.

When you arrive at the Omelette Parlor, the hostess seats you at a small table in a quiet corner. Richard helps you off with your coat.

"I'll keep the scarf on," you say, feeling deceitful.

"This is so nice," Richard says, stretching his

(continued on page 50)

arms and leaning back. "I feel as though I haven't relaxed in weeks. Ever since I started reporting, I can't seem to sit down."

"Why are you always running? Don't you have specific hours?" you ask.

"Well, it's kind of a long story. Three of us were hired as trial interns during this vacation. One of us will be kept on for the rest of the year. It's pretty heavy-duty competition."

"So you're hustling. Is that what the beeper is all about?"

"Yep. I have this deal with a copyboy at the paper. Whenever anything interesting comes over the police radio, he beeps me. I spend half my life chasing dead-end stories; but I just know that if I keep running, something will pay off. The problem is that I constantly get beeped."

"I've noticed!" you say, finding it hard to be angry at him.

"Excuse me, ma'am," says a waiter, interrupting your thought. "You have a phone call. The woman says it's urgent."

Oh, no. It's Karen! You completely forgot about your plan. You rush over to the phone.

"You're kidding! Yes, I will. Okay. Thanks for calling." Karen is talking gibberish on the other end. You fight off laughter.

"I'll see you in a few minutes. Good luck!" she says.

(continued on page 51)

You hang up and return to the table. Richard stands up anxiously. "Is everything all right? Is there anything I can do?"

You look helplessly into his concerned eyes.

If you follow through with the plan and leave, turn to page 32.

If you decide you'd rather stay, turn to page 43.

You pull yourself along the rail until you reach the exit.

I hope they don't see us, you think, wishing you were invisible.

You keep your head down and slip off the ice at the nearest opening. Karen follows. You waddle behind the wall and find your way to a bench.

After returning your skates, you and Karen rush up the stairs, past the giant Christmas tree, through the crowds, and around the corner toward Fifth Avenue.

"Phew!" Karen says. "We made it!"

"That was a close one!" you say as you walk up the street.

Two girls walk past you with skates over their shoulders. "This is going to be so much fun," one of them says.

Suddenly you feel a twinge. *It could have been fun for us, too,* you think. *Why couldn't we have enjoyed ourselves anyway?*

"You know," Karen says, "why do guys have so much control over us?"

"I don't know," you say. But then you think about it. *Because we give it to them,* you say to yourself.

The End

You are about to accept Craig's invitation when LBF comes storming out your door. Before you know it, she is in Craig's kitchen whirling in battle with another white ball of fluff. Both dogs are growling fiercely.

"I'm sorry," you say, wondering if you can run into Craig's house after LBF.

Instead, Craig goes after the tiny nondog dogs and picks both of them up in a lump. He passes LBF over to you.

"I think that's a sign that you have to join us for lunch," he says.

"Either that, or a sign that I'll be in trouble if I do." You laugh. "But I think I'll take my chances. I'd love to help you test those recipes. Thanks for inviting me."

"Terrific," he says. "Come on in. I'm just getting the ingredients set for the main course."

You run back inside to tell Karen to forget about calling you at the restaurant, and to let her know where you'll be. Karen has a play rehearsal this afternoon.

"My luck," she says. "I'm taking a peanut butter and jelly sandwich with me. Have fun."

You return to the back door and enter Craig's kitchen. You cannot believe what you see. You feel as though you are in the kitchen of a restaurant. The stove is stainless steel and has eight burners and two giant ovens. There is a built-in charcoal grill that vents out a window, copper and stainless pots hang-

(continued on page 54)

ing from the ceiling, and an unbelievable array of knives magnetized onto a wall fixture. On a huge island in the middle of the kitchen is a second sink and more counter space than you have ever seen.

"Wow," you say. "This is incredible!"

"It's my classroom," he says. "I plan someday to own the finest restaurant in New York City." He points to a chair. "Make yourself comfortable. I still have some assembling to do."

You sit quietly and watch him work. He is very intense about everything he does; there is passion in his eyes. You watch as he chops some vegetables with rhythmic, staccato movements; you are impressed by the gracefulness and ease with which he wraps pieces of meat in a pastry dough and places them in the oven. And finally you watch him toss some strange-looking clumps of reddish meat into a cast-iron skillet.

"I'm ready," he says moments later. "Come in the other room and meet my mother and her friend."

After the introductions, you all walk to the dining room. The table is elegantly set, with delicate china and cut-glass candlesticks. You don't know whether to keep exclaiming how wonderful it all is or to pretend that you always live this way. You decide to play it down.

"What a beautiful table," you say softly, in what you hope is a sophisticated tone. What you really want to do is yell, "Oh, my God! This is incredible! I can't believe I'm here! I think I am falling in love!"

(continued on page 55)

"Be right back with the first course," says Craig, and he disappears into the kitchen.

He reappears seconds later with four plates on a tray. Each plate has several little lumps of brown in the middle and some sprigs of something green on the side.

"Cervelle de veau au beurre noir," says Craig as he places the first course in front of you.

"I'm afraid I'm taking Spanish. Can you please translate for me?" you say, preferring to be honest rather than to pretend.

He smiles as he picks up his fork. "Calves' brains in burnt butter." He takes a bite.

Your stomach flips at the word *brains*. You suddenly feel a wave of nausea. *There is no way I can eat the brains of a calf,* you think. *No way.*

If you give it a try, turn to page 79.

If you don't, turn to page 85.

"I just want to go home!" you say. "I've never been so humiliated in my whole life! How could he?"

Tears are streaming down your face. Karen puts her arm around you.

"It's all right. Other singers have had shorter careers," she says.

"But not more embarrassing!" you say. "All those people!"

You arrive home and throw yourself down on the couch. Karen dumps out your guitar case. Thirty-eight dollars," she says. "That's more than we made the other day. And the hours were shorter."

"Yeah, sure," you say. "I'm never speaking to him again."

You turn on the TV. Both of you are in rotten moods, and you barely talk.

About an hour later the phone rings.

"Hello," you grumble.

"Don't hang up. It's Bobby," says your brother.

"I have nothing to say to you," you say. "Haven't you caused enough damage already?"

"That's why I'm calling," he says in a warm voice. "I'm sorry. I thought about what I did and I was wrong. I overreacted. I guess I just couldn't deal with seeing my little sister out there. I got worried."

You say nothing.

"Listen," he says. "If you and Karen want to play, go ahead. But I want to ask you a favor. Will you

(continued on page 57)

give me your schedule so that I can hang around in the area? I won't even talk to you."

Bobby has never apologized to you for anything before in his life. Nor has he ever demonstrated so clearly how much he really cares.

"Okay," you say. "I'll call you."

By the time you hang up the phone, tears are spilling down your cheeks. This time, though, they are tears of love.

The End

"No way!" you both say in unison.

As you walk up the street, Karen turns to you and announces, "When I'm a rich and famous actress, I will give you free tickets to all my shows."

"Thanks," you say, smiling.

You leisurely walk back up Fifth Avenue toward the apartment, looking at all the Christmas windows and fighting through hordes of last-minute shoppers.

"Just think," you say. "We can just go back, sit, relax and there is no one to nag us about anything. Just us!"

"I love it!" shouts Karen to the world. Heads turn to look at her.

"Nut!" you say, punching her in the shoulder.

When you get out of the elevator on your floor, you discover a petite, brown-haired girl sitting on the floor in front of your door.

"Sarah!" you say. "What are you doing here?"

Sarah is your mother's best friend's daughter. You have known her since you were three years old when you went to nursery school together. You and she have spent a lot of time together over the years . . . vacations, visits, schools, parties. Unfortunately, the two of you have never really hit it off. You don't dislike her, but you have nothing in common. When you wanted to play in the park, Sarah wanted to go to the museum; if you wanted a hot dog, Sarah wanted soup; if you wanted to stay up late or read under the covers, Sarah was always tired.

Sarah's mother, Ann, however, is another story.

(continued on page 59)

You absolutely adore Ann. She is warm, fun, easy to talk to. You've always had a special relationship with her. In fact, it was always easier to ask Ann for advice on boys than it was to ask your mother.

Ann sometimes asks your advice, too. The day before you came to the Gordons, Ann told you that Sarah has been dating a guy whom Ann can't stand. Ann wondered what she, as a mother, should do. You told her to stay out of it; Sarah was going to have to work it out for herself. You knew that if Ann insisted Sarah stop dating this guy, Sarah would rebel.

You are amazed to see Sarah at your doorstep.

"So what's up?" you ask Sarah as you all go inside. "How are you?"

"Oh, I'm fine," she says. "I . . . uh . . . my mother told me you were here." Sarah doesn't look straight at you. She looks at the floor, at the wall, around the room. "Uh . . . can I have a glass of water?"

"Sure," you say, a bit perplexed by her nervousness. You go into the kitchen.

"Listen," she says. "You guys are here alone, right?"

You nod.

"Well, could I crash here for a while?" Sarah asks.

Your eyes nearly pop. You look at Karen. She has the same expression on her face.

What do I do? you think. You and Karen have

(continued on page 60)

waited so long to have this time together . . . alone.
If Sarah stays, you will have to include her in everything you do.

How could this be happening? you think.

You look at Karen. You look at Sarah.

If you tell Sarah that she can stay, turn to page 69.

If you give her an excuse why she can't, turn to page 75.

"Let's just have fun," you say. "We're already here. I'm sure there are a million cute guys on this ice just dying to meet us."

"Right," says Karen. "Let's start by getting up."

"Excuse me," says a tall slim woman, nearly falling over you as she skates by backward. She is wearing a tiny bright blue skating skirt and a leotard and tights to match.

You grab on to the rail and pull yourself up. A woman with a fur coat skates smoothly by. A boy just a little older than you, wearing dark-blue stretch pants, practices spins in the middle of the rink, while a girl twirls by in a sequined outfit. A mother skates backward pulling a little girl that can't be more than three years old. A five-year-old whizzes by you.

You look at Karen and begin to laugh. She is standing at the edge next to you, holding on to the rail with both hands. She is wearing baggy Levi's and a bulky sweater. You have on so many layers that you can barely move.

"As you know," Karen says, "the really good skaters don't have to show off by their fancy clothes."

You laugh. "Right!" you say. "We do it by our skating."

Out of the corner of your eye, you see Greg and Jon still standing with the two blondes. "Come on," you say. "Let's try."

You take a step away from the rail and stand still.

(continued on page 62)

Karen follows. You slide a bit farther out, carefully balancing yourself, arms straight out as if you were on a tightrope.

"Watch out!" a boy yells as he shoots by, knocking your arm.

Your feet slide out from under you and you grab Karen's arm for support. You both scream and tumble down onto the ice.

"What did you think I was going to do?" Karen says. You both laugh.

You balance on each other and try to stand up. You are concentrating intensely.

"They're coming!" Karen yells, and she grabs your arm. Once again you tumble to the ice in a heap. This time you duck your heads and try not to laugh.

The foursome skate by, involved in their own activity, never noticing you. You and Karen look at each other and break into a fit of giggles. Then you actually get up and start skating, slowly and awkwardly, but upright.

Karen is squealing behind you. "Wait for me!"

"No, I can't stop!" you say, trying to turn around to see Karen.

A girl skates gracefully by you, crossing one leg over the other and gliding into a spin as she nears the middle.

"Looks kind of like me, huh?" you say, turning to see Karen. Just then you spot Jon coming up behind Karen. He is alone.

(continued on page 63)

"Karen!" you shout. "Behind you!"

She turns around and one leg flies out from under her and she lands flat on her back, sprawled out on the ice.

"Hey, don't I know you?" Jon says, stopping short next to you and spraying you with ice.

"Uh . . ." you begin, suddenly losing your balance and landing on the ice. *I have never been so embarrassed,* you think, struggling to catch your composure.

"Let me help you!" Jon says, holding out his hand. You grab it and he lifts you up.

"So how are you?" you say, trying to ignore the fact that you just fell flat on your face in front of him.

"Hi," Karen says, skating awkwardly up to you. You cannot control yourself and you burst out laughing.

"Don't make me . . ." Karen squeals. But it is too late. She grabs on to your shoulder, you grab on to Jon's, and the three of you tumble to the ground.

"You two cause more trouble," he says, laughing.

"Well, what do we have here!" Greg says, skating up and covering all of you in spray. The two girls are skating behind him. You look at the expressions on their faces and want to die.

And we can't even skate away, you think.

Greg holds his hand out to Karen and helps her up. Jon picks you up.

The girls are going to love that! you think.

You and Karen look helplessly at each other.

(continued on page 64)

"Well, fancy meeting you here!" says Greg. "Hey, Jon, that was a pretty tricky step; you'll have to teach me that one."

"Right, Greg!" Jon says. The taller blond girl is staring right at you. You feel very uncomfortable. You stare at the ground, the other skaters, Karen.

How can we get out of here? you think.

"Oh, I'm sorry. I haven't introduced you," Jon says. "This is my sister, Polly, and Greg's sister, Jenny."

You are speechless. You look at Karen. There is a smirk on her face and a gleam in her eyes.

"Nice to meet you," you say.

"Come on," Jon says, taking your hand. "I think you need a lesson."

You glance at Karen. She is leaning against Greg, trying to get her balance, smiling broadly.

The End

"I still think we should go skating," Karen says on the way home.

"Another time," you say, absentmindedly.

"Another time?" says Karen. "Another time? Are you nuts?"

When you get back to the apartment, you find a note in the living room from the Gordons with house instructions. Stuff about how to use the dishwasher, how to water the plants and feed the dogs and put out the garbage. Folded in the note is an envelope marked SPERLING.

You look back at the instruction sheet. The final item reads:

> *We have promised to leave these tickets to the musical* Glories at Noon *at the box office for our friends. We would really appreciate it if you would drop them by the Corliss Theatre for us by Saturday. Thank you and have fun!*
> *Love,*
> *Mary and Stan*

Karen is reading over your shoulder. "Oh, let me hold those." She takes the tickets out of the envelope and caresses them as though they were precious jewels. "I wish they were for us! I've been dying to see *Glories* since the day it opened. It's the hottest musical to hit Broadway in years. I would do *anything* to see that show!"

Karen is melodramatic about everything. She is

(continued on page 66)

an actress and loves to play the stereotypical over-emotional star.

"Look at this," she says, pointing to the ticket price of forty-five dollars. "Maybe the Sperlings will get sick. Maybe I will kill them." She throws her arms in the air.

"Do they have half-price tickets?" you ask.

"I doubt it, but we could check when we're there. Then again, maybe we could sneak in the back way. I'll just tell them I'm the pianist in the orchestra."

Karen walks over to the beautiful grand piano in the living room and begins to play a song from *La Cage aux Folles*. "I am what I am, and I am . . ." Her deep, resonant voice fills the room. You run into the hall, grab your guitar, and begin to sing and play.

When the song is over, Karen jumps up on the piano bench. "The Twintones, ladies and gentlemen. Let's hear it for the Twintones. Hey, that's a great name for us. Let's do another one."

You play and sing and dance for the next two hours, lost in the reverie of your music, in the excitement of being able to do anything you want. By the time you stop, you are both exhausted and starved.

"Let's check out the refrigerator," you say, knowing that the Gordons must have left stuff.

You find cold chicken and plenty of vegetables for a salad. After you eat, you go back to the piano and play until you collapse.

(continued on page 67)

The next day you and Karen walk down to the theater district.

"Broadway, here we come!" shouts Karen. "I hope we don't get mobbed by autograph seekers."

When you reach the theater, you notice a man playing a Beatles' song on the guitar. He is standing just outside the door and there is an open guitar case in front of him. There are dollar bills and change in the case.

"We're much better," you say to Karen as you walk into the lobby.

There is a line at the box office where you are supposed to leave the tickets. As you wait you hear the person behind the window telling people that the show is sold out until the end of February.

"See," says Karen. "Even if we had the money, we couldn't get a ticket. So much for our theater-going."

You drop the tickets off and walk toward the door.

"I have two extra tickets for today's performance," says a man in a suit. "You can have them for what I paid."

A woman approaches you. "My husband is ill. Would you like to buy a ticket for tonight?"

"No, thanks," you say. Then you turn to Karen. "I bet this happens at every performance. We could get tickets if we had money."

"I guess you're right," says Karen. "But we don't have money."

(continued on page 68)

You walk outside and discover that a young guy with a violin is playing across from the guitarist.

"I wonder how much those guys make?" you say.

"Look at all the money in their cases," Karen says. "People who go to the theater are rich."

The sidewalk is crowded with people . . . some are just standing there; others are going in to the matinee performance. You stop for a while to listen to the violinist.

Suddenly you turn to look at Karen. She is looking at you. You both smile nervously.

"Could we?" you say.

"Would we?" she says.

If you do, turn to page 89.

If you don't, turn to page 58.

"Uh . . . yeah, sure," you say. *How could I say no,* you think.

"Oh, thank you!" she says, suddenly smiling. "I'll go get my stuff and be back in a while." She hugs you and runs out the door.

Dumbfounded, you look at Karen. "What could I say?"

"Exactly what you did," Karen says. "It's all right. She seems nice."

"Yeah," you say. "She is."

"Let's make a big dinner tonight for the three of us," Karen says. "That'll be fun."

You and Karen pull out three cookbooks and leaf through them.

"Spaghetti with meat sauce," Karen suggests.

"Teriyaki steak," you say.

Finally you decide on chicken curry. You make a grocery list and write a quick note for Sarah. Then you and Karen head for the market.

When you get back, there is no sign of Sarah.

"Let's get started," you say. "I think we have to wash the chicken."

"Why would you wash a chicken?" Karen asks.

"I don't know; my mother washes hers," you say.

By five-thirty the curry is almost ready and you are starving. Still no sign of Sarah.

"We can't put the rice on until Sarah gets home," you say. "She should have been here long ago."

Just then you hear the elevator, and there is a knock on the door. You open it and find Sarah

(continued on page 70)

standing next to a tall brown-haired guy wearing blue jeans and a jeans jacket.

"Hi," you say hesitantly.

"This is Peter," Sarah says.

"How's it going?" he says, and walks in. "Something smells real good."

He walks in the kitchen and takes the lid off the pot. You look at Karen. She shrugs her shoulders.

"Do you mind if we join you for dinner?" Sarah asks.

"Of course not. We had planned on you being here. I just didn't know you were going to bring Peter."

"I'm sorry, but these days are our only time to be together. My mom won't let me see him," she says angrily. Her whole body tenses as she speaks.

You say nothing. Suddenly you feel uneasy.

"I better check on dinner," you blurt out, looking to see if the rice water is boiling.

Peter picks up the phone that is next to the stove. "Hey, can I use the phone?" You nod.

"Hey, Jimmy. What's up?" Peter says into the receiver. "I won't be able to make it tonight; I'm having dinner with three chicks." He hangs up.

You cannot believe what he just said.

"Listen," you say to Sarah and Peter, "why don't you guys go relax? We'll call you when dinner's ready."

Karen pulls you over to the corner.

(continued on page 71)

"I can't believe the nerve of that guy," she says. "When you were talking to Sarah, he opened the fridge and asked if we had any beer. I told him that if we did, it wasn't for him to drink."

"What does she see in him?" you ask.

"Ya got me," says Karen.

After setting the table with little dishes of chopped cucumber, peanuts, raisins, coconut, and chutney, you call Sarah and Peter in.

All through dinner Peter talks about how good he is at playing pool and the trouble he's gotten into lately with his friends. You and Karen barely say a word; and you can sense that even Sarah feels uneasy.

After eating at least three helpings, Peter immediately asks what is for dessert. You are ready to kill him.

When you bring out the ice cream, he demolishes three bowls full. You feel sick to your stomach watching him.

"Come on," he says to Sarah a short while later. "I told Tony that we'd meet him at the pool hall at nine. You girls want to come?"

"No, thanks!" you say.

You give Sarah a key and tell her to be careful.

For the next three days you barely see Sarah. She leaves in the morning and usually doesn't come home during the day. She is always with Peter.

You just don't understand why she likes him. He

(continued on page 72)

is the rudest guy you have ever met. One night he called at two A.M. to talk to Sarah.

You wonder if you should call Sarah's mother, but you have a feeling that that would be the worst thing to do at this point.

The morning of the fourth day, you, Karen, and Sarah have breakfast together. Every day you have asked Sarah if she wanted to join you. She has always said no. Today she asks you if she can. She seems depressed.

The phone rings and Sarah jumps. "I'm not here," she says.

It's Peter, and you tell him that Sarah has left. When you hang up the phone, you look at Sarah.

"What happened?" you ask.

"Nothing," she says. "I don't know. I just can't deal with him anymore." A tear runs down her cheek. "I don't know why I liked him. I don't even know if I ever did. I just know that I never want to see him again!"

You put your arm around her. "It doesn't matter, as long as you realize it now," you say.

"Thanks," she says. "I think that when my mother told me I couldn't see Peter, it just made me want to more. I guess I needed to find out for myself."

You feel very close to Sarah. She has never opened up in this way to you before.

"I know!" Karen says. "Let's go to the Bronx

(continued on page 73)

Zoo today. We'll get you cheered up in no time!" she says to Sarah.

"That sounds great," Sarah says. "Thanks, you guys. I don't know what I would have done if you hadn't been here for me."

Tears are streaming down your cheeks. You definitely made the right decision this time!

The End

What's life without risk? you decide.

You walk casually toward the ramp, trying not to stare at this guy. Carefully you step up, holding the glue tightly.

It's sturdy, you decide, taking two more steps up the incline. *No problem.*

Slowly you edge your way up the ramp, which is actually a board about a foot wide. You glance up at the guy. *He's like a movie star,* you think. *Maybe he is! I am in Los Angeles.*

Suddenly you lose your footing. You feel yourself going down, and the pail flies into the air. When you and the pail are finally settled, you are completely covered with thick, mucky glue. You are humiliated. You wish you could disappear.

Then, out of nowhere, Mark and Bob appear with a pail of petals, which they carefully place, one by one, on your glued body. They are doubled over in hysterics. You look at them; you look at yourself. And instead of crying, you laugh.

The End

"Listen, Sarah," you say, taking a deep breath. "I promised the Gordons that it would only be me and Karen staying here. You can visit us any time you want, but I'd feel a little funny letting you stay over. I mean, they really trusted me."

"Sure. I understand," Sarah says in a stiff voice. Her face has no expression.

"I'm sorry," you say, wishing you could disappear. "Why don't you have dinner with us?"

"No, thanks. I better get moving. Oh, can I use your phone?" Sarah stares at the floor.

You walk her into the kitchen and she dials a number.

"Hi," she says in a very low voice, almost covering her mouth. You walk into the hall.

"No," Sarah says. "I don't know . . . Yes . . . Okay, I'll be there in twenty minutes. Bye."

She walks into the hall. "Well, nice seeing you. Have fun," she says to you.

"Sarah, I'm really sorry," you say, suddenly feeling lousy.

"Bye!" she says, and walks out the door. You stand there for a minute, silent.

"Now I feel really bad!" you say.

"Hey, don't worry about it. So, she goes home; she'll live," Karen reassures you. "What would we have done with her?"

"Yeah, I guess you're right," you say.

"We'll go have dinner somewhere tonight and for-

(continued on page 76)

get about it," Karen says. "I know! Let's order Chinese food."

"Yum!" you say, putting Sarah out of your mind.

For the next two days you and Karen run around nonstop. You go to the American Museum of Natural History, the Children's Zoo in Central Park, and the Museum of Modern Art. On the third day you jog in the park and then make a big spaghetti dinner with ice cream sundaes for dessert.

"You want to know how you tell if the spaghetti is ready?" Karen asks. "You throw a piece of spaghetti on the ceiling. If it sticks, it's cooked!"

"You're crazy!" you say.

"Well, it works," she says. "But I guess you could just taste it." You both laugh.

The phone rings and Karen answers it.

"Just a minute," she says, handing the phone to you.

"Oh, hi, Ann! How are you?" you say. It is Sarah's mother. She sounds horrible and her voice cracks as she speaks.

"She what?" you say, suddenly feeling your knees go weak.

Sarah has run away.

"She had told me she was going to stay with you. And that's where I thought she was . . . . until an hour ago. I just found out she's with him . . . Peter. And she has been for the last three days."

You try to understand what has happened, but your mind is whirling. You've never heard Ann like

(continued on page 77)

this before. Peter is Sarah's boyfriend. The last time you spoke to Ann, she described him as rude, obnoxious, and a troublemaker.

"Did she ever come there? Do you know where she might be? Do you know anything?" Ann says frantically.

You know nothing.

Ann reads you a letter that she received an hour ago.

> *"Dear Mom and Dad,*
>   *I just want you to know that I am all right. I'm with Peter and I'm sorry that I had to do this, but you just don't understand me. I need to have some freedom for a while.*
>   *Please don't worry.*
>   *Love,*
>   *Sarah"*

You feel a knot in your stomach. She came to you and you turned her away.

The End

You look at Dan. You look at Maria. You look at all the unfamiliar faces. *No way,* you think.

"I'll go," you say, standing up.

Dan looks at you, surprised and disappointed. "I'd like to get your address," he says.

"Come on," Kevin yells. "Let's go."

"When we get back," you say, running out.

"Sure," says Dan, half to himself, half to you.

The next party is more of the same: fancy cars, loud music, and hundreds of people.

You have been at the party for less than an hour when all of a sudden a helicopter roars overhead and shines a spotlight into the yard.

"Everyone, please leave," announces a loud-speaker. Police file in and the partiers head back to their cars. You have never seen anything like it. Maria explains that a lot of big parties are broken up because of complaints from neighbors.

As you are climbing into Maria's car, she shakes you and points to two guys about to turn the corner, "It's him! The one on the left is in my gym class and I've been staring at him all year. I have to know where he lives. Let's follow them."

You were hoping to go back and see Dan.

If you follow the guys, turn to page 86.

If you go back, turn to page 19.

You cannot believe that you are about to bite into a brain. You visualize the lumpy, grayish-reddish brain in formaldehyde that was passed around in biology last year. You couldn't even look at it, let alone eat it!

Well, here goes, you say to yourself as you put a forkful into your mouth. You try to block off your nose so that you won't taste it. It's a trick you learned with cough medicine when you were a kid.

Slowly and deliberately you chew the little piece in your mouth. Then you pick up the water and gulp the mouthful down.

So far, so good, you think. Then you look at Craig. He is waiting for a comment. His mother and her friend have already said that they think it is superb.

You smile. You cannot bring yourself to lie.

"I've never had anything like this!" you say, non-committally. "It's a totally new experience for me. This is exciting."

In a nauseating sort of way, you think. Then you dip a small piece of bread in the sauce and pop it into your mouth.

"The sauce is wonderful!" you say honestly.

How am I going to get through the rest of this? you wonder. And just then a miracle in the form of a fluffy white dog rubs against your foot. Carefully watching the eyes and attention of the others at the table, you manage to slip the remaining three pieces to the dog, unnoticed. You feel her tongue licking

(continued on page 80)

the sauce off of your fingers after she has eaten the brains. *The worst is over,* you think, knowing that the next course is lamb in a pastry crust. You sigh in relief.

The rest of the meal is fantastic, and with every bite your crush on Craig gets bigger. You love the pride he feels in his work; you love his manners, his gentleness, his sophistication. And the fact that he is so smashingly good-looking with that soft, wavy dark-brown hair and those deep, wonderful eyes doesn't hurt a bit.

When lunch is over, you all sit in the living room. Marcia, the friend, snuggles into a big arm chair and tells Craig how extraordinary she thought the meal was.

"Now, if we just had some quiet, classical guitar for an after-lunch interlude, the experience would be perfection," she says.

Your heart jumps. Less than fifty feet away, on the other side of the wall, is your guitar; and you have been playing classical music since you were ten years old.

If you offer to get your guitar and play, turn to page 99.

If you are too shy, turn to page 104.

"Let's get out of here," you say, and you and Maria find your way to an exit.

The next few days are packed. You drive to Malibu, spend a day at Disneyland, roller-skate on the Venice boardwalk, and have a dinner of raw fish wrapped in seaweed . . . *sushi,* they call it. You spend fifteen minutes staring at this strange food and insisting that there is no way you are going to like it. When you finally taste it, you are too embarrassed to admit that it is actually good.

After your sushi dinner Thursday night, you and Maria pack for Mexico. You are so excited that you cannot sleep.

The horn honks at eleven. You and Maria rush out. You climb in next to Bob in the backseat. Maria follows you. Pete and Mark are in the front.

"The Markmobile is loaded and ready for take-off," says Mark, pulling out of the driveway.

"A Mexico we go, a Mexico we go . . ." sings Bob.

"Fish tacos!" Pete says.

"Sounds disgusting," you say.

"No way," says Bob. "They're the best!"

The drive to the border is two and a half hours long. There is not a moment of silence. The guys are crazy, and they keep you and Maria laughing all the way. Every ten minutes one of the guys tells a Bruce joke.

"How many Bruces does it take to screw in a light bulb?" Bob asks.

(continued on page 82)

"I give up," you say.

"Two. One to hold the light bulb and another to turn him." The guys burst out laughing.

It is not until you are halfway there that you discover that Bruce is Mark's sixteen-year-old brother. *Must be a loser,* you think.

When you arrive at the Mexican border, Mark becomes serious. "Okay, everyone. Mellow out! Let's get through Tijuana without any trouble."

"Oh, Mark. Get a grip. We never cause trouble," says Bob. He leans over and tickles you. You laugh and hit him back. There is something about Bob that really appeals to you: a certain self-assurance, to say nothing of his sparkling blue eyes.

"Come on, guys," Mark says. "This is serious."

You drive up to a man in a uniform. He waves you on.

"That's it?" you ask.

"That's it," says Mark. "Now we have a detour through the center of Tijuana."

You stare out the window in shock. You have never seen poverty like this: The buildings are shacks that look as if they have been thrown together with glue; and the people are dressed in rags. Even the dogs look as though they are starving.

Finally you turn down a curvy road filled with potholes. "This is it," says Mark. "The main road to Rosarita. Welcome to Mexico!"

About twenty minutes later you stop at a small restaurant overlooking the ocean. "The best chips

(continued on page 83)

and guacamole in the world," announces Bob. After eating them, you agree.

Then it's back in the car for the last lap. Mark finally announces that you have arrived at the trailer camp where his family rents a home overlooking the ocean. The sun is setting as you pull up, and the spectacular orange sky is the backdrop for the roaring ocean waves.

A short, thin woman walks over to the car as you are piling out. "Greetings," she says, warmly welcoming you all.

"Hi," says a boy, tall with sandy, streaked hair. It's Bruce. He has a young face, but looks friendly and kind of cute.

Why all the Bruce jokes? you wonder.

That night the guys cook a wonderful barbecue dinner. Afterward, all of you, including Mark's mother, go dancing at a nearby hotel. A mariachi band blares its beat and you go wild on the dance floor.

You spend most of the night dancing with either Bob or Mark. They keep cutting in on each other. "This is my dance!" screams one, grabbing you by one arm. "Oh, no, it's mine," says the other, hanging on to your other arm. At first you enjoy the attention; but after a while you are ready to scream.

The next day you and Maria wake up early. "Pete wanted to go for a long walk this morning," she says. "Do you mind?"

You do; but you look at her glowing face. "Of course not," you say.

(continued on page 84)

You throw on a sweatshirt and walk outside. The waves are breaking against the shore and the air is crisp and moist.

"Good morning!" says Mark, joining you. "It's supposed to be seventy-seven degrees today. You up for a beach day?"

"Sounds good," you say.

"No way," says Bob, walking up. "She's coming horseback riding with me."

"She wants to sit on the beach," says Mark.

"She'll do that tomorrow," says Bob. "She'd rather ride today."

You are sick and tired of being told what you want to do and you are about to tell both of them off when Bruce marches up.

"Anyone want to go to Ensenada with me?" he asks.

Escape, you think, amused by the idea of leaving Bob and Mark to argue with each other.

If you go to Ensenada with Bruce, turn to page 11.

If you try to settle with Bob and Mark, turn to page 95.

You swallow hard and think again about eating brains. You know that you cannot do it. You also know that Craig will be very disappointed.

You are right. When you say that you cannot bring yourself to eat brains, the sparkle goes out of his eyes. He is polite. He says that he understands, but it is very clear to you that anyone who does not share his love and passion for food will never be an important part of his life.

He is one of the most interesting boys you have ever met, and you have just eliminated him from your life because you didn't have the courage to try something new.

The End

The guys turn the corner and Maria pulls out with her lights off. They take a left on the next street. Maria waits and then takes a left, too.

"Be careful. Don't get too close!" you say.

They turn left; Maria follows. "I feel like a spy!" she says.

Suddenly there is a siren behind you. Maria pulls over and two policemen walk up to Maria's window. One flashes a light into the car.

"Young lady, do you realize you are driving down a one-way street the wrong way . . . without lights?"

"No, sir," says Maria. "I'm sorry."

The policeman writes out a ticket and leaves. That's when you notice the two guys standing on the sidewalk, watching everything. *How embarrassing!*

"Hi, girls," the tall one says, smirking. Then he looks at Maria. "Say, aren't you in my gym class?"

You are ready to die. "I think so," says Maria, poking you.

"Well," says the other guy, "you girls seem to be having a bad night. We're on our way to get some ice cream. Can we buy you some?"

"Sure!" Maria says. "Hop in!"

At least it isn't a total disaster, you think.

The End

"Let's go!" you say, and grab Maria's hand. You run through the door without looking back.

You hear a voice ahead of you and duck behind a curtain. Your heart is pounding. You peek out. The hall is clear.

"This way," Maria says, walking quickly down the hall. "Act calm, like we belong."

A woman in a funky glitter top walks by. She smiles. You smile back.

"Hi," you manage to say, and you walk on.

Two guys are talking animatedly as they pass you. They don't even look. You keep going.

"It's over here," says Maria. You keep following her. Now there are other people around. You try to look as though you are part of them.

"We made it!" says Maria, stopping just in front of a dressing room.

"Hey, you two girls! Get back here!" the guard yells. He is walking straight toward you.

Suddenly the dressing room door opens and Bruce Wintersteen walks out.

You look at the guard. You look at Wintersteen. You had told the guard that Wintersteen invited you to come backstage.

"We're dead," Maria whispers. "We're absolutely dead."

The guard walks over. He yells loudly, "I thought I told you girls to leave. Now, get moving! I know you don't know anyone back here!"

(continued on page 88)

"What's all the ruckus?" someone says. You turn around to face Bruce Wintersteen. Two feet away!

"Sorry about that," says the guard. "These girls said they knew you and they sneaked . . ."

You close your eyes. *How embarrassing!* you think.

Suddenly Bruce puts his arm around you. "They do know me," he says. Your eyes nearly pop out. "In fact, they're close friends of mine." He kisses you on the cheek. *You could die!*

"Sorry," says the guard. He leaves.

Bruce smiles at you and leads you into the dressing room. It is filled with band people, managers, friends, and press. You are so overwhelmed that you cannot speak.

"Why don't you have something to eat?" he says, leading you to the buffet table. He squeezes your arm, smiles, and walks away.

The End

"Why not?" Karen says.

"Well, I could start with what our mothers would do to us if they found out," you say.

"Nobody's going to see us," Karen says. "Let's. Oh, come on."

Your heart is pounding. You feel a rush of adrenaline, a sense of scared excitement. "Yes, yes! Let's do it!" you scream. And the two of you practically run all the way home.

"Hey, hey, we're the Twintones!" Karen sings to the tune of the Monkees' theme song.

For the next two days you practice nonstop.

"If we're going to go out there and play, we're going to do it well," Karen insists.

You finally work out a medley of songs in which you play the guitar and Karen sings. You back her up with harmony. You also practice some songs from old musicals like *Oklahoma!* and *West Side Story,* and some newer ones from *Cats* and *La Cage aux Folles.* Then you throw in some Christmas tunes and dig up some bells to ring.

Finally, on the third day of practicing, Karen suggests that you do your first performance at a Wednesday matinee.

"I can't believe we're doing this!" you say over and over again Wednesday morning. "I know we're nuts!" You can feel the butterflies in your stomach.

On your way to the theater you pass an old man playing the flute by the Plaza Hotel. You both look at him.

(continued on page 90)

"Can we go home now?" you say, stopping. Karen drags you down the street.

When you get to the theater, the street is quiet. You had decided to get there by twelve-thirty so you could prepare yourselves. The matinee begins at two o'clock.

"Okay, here we are," you say to Karen. "Here we are in front of a theater."

"Yep! Here we are," she says. "Now what?"

"Let's start playing before I have time to think. My nerve is going fast."

You begin to tune your guitar when a bearded man with a guitar around his neck walks over to you.

"Hi, girls. What are you doing?"

"Oh, playing a few songs," you say.

"Well, listen," he says. "I'm going to ask you a favor. I've been playing this spot for two years and I would appreciate it if you played somewhere else."

"Uh . . . sure . . . okay," you say.

"There hasn't been anyone at the theater across the street for a while," he says. "Why don't you try over there?"

"Sure," Karen says. "Thanks."

The man holds out his hand. "My name's Keith," he says. "Welcome. I think you'll find this a good place to play. People who come to the theater are in a festive, happy, generous mood. But the big money is at night. That's when you get the big spenders. Christmas is the best season of the year, too. Good luck."

(continued on page 91)

You and Karen thank him and cross the street. About five minutes later you are ready to play. People are still straggling by. The big crowds haven't arrived yet.

"What should we play?" you say.

"Let's play a *Cats* song. How about 'Memories'?"

"Okay!" You take a deep breath. "Here goes nothing."

Your hand is shaking. You play a few chords; Karen hums a few bars and then begins singing.

The beginning is a bit awkward. Karen is too soft and you are playing as though you are not sure what chord comes next. But after a few beats, you are together and strong.

A woman stops and listens. You smile. She walks on.

A couple stops. The man shakes his head to the music. "I loved that show," the woman says. She throws fifty cents into your guitar case.

Suddenly you are no longer nervous. In fact, by the time you play your third song, you are actually enjoying yourself. It's as though an imaginary person has taken over your hands, your body.

The matinee crowd begins to arrive. Couples, foursomes, threesomes. Many stop to listen.

"Hey, you're pretty good!" a man says, dropping a dollar in your case. Others toss in quarters, dimes.

"Now, what are two beautiful girls like you doing out here?" an older man says. "You should be inside on stage."

(continued on page 92)

"I agree," Karen says, interrupting the song for a moment. A few people laugh.

At two-fifteen you decide to quit. The only people left are late for the show and they are rushing inside.

"Look!" you say, pointing to all the money in your case.

"Let's not count it till we get home!" Karen says. "Can you believe we just did that? It was fun!"

You are both bubbling over.

You get home and dump all the money onto the floor. Karen starts counting change. You count the bills.

"A five-dollar bill!" you shout. "Someone gave us five dollars!" You dance around, waving the bill.

The total comes to twenty-six dollars and forty-three cents. You both jump up and down and decide that your next trip will be the big time: Saturday night.

You practice constantly for the next few days and Saturday comes quickly. You catch the bus down Fifth Avenue and walk across to the theater. As you are setting up, you see Keith across the street. You wave. He smiles and waves back.

"Good to see you again!" he yells.

"You, too," Karen says.

Once again you quickly get involved in your music, only this time, it's twice as exciting. The theater lights sparkle; people dressed in tuxes and sequined gowns pour out of taxi cabs and stretch limousines. The whole scene is so overwhelming and thrilling

(continued on page 93)

that a wonderful energy surges through your body as the music flows out of you.

People stop and talk to you, clap for you, and of course, toss money into your case. You are bursting with the excitement of it all. You cannot stop smiling.

Two younger couples sing "Santa Claus Is Coming to Town" with you. You all dance in a circle, laughing and singing together.

"What are you doing!" a loud harsh voice suddenly yells.

You look over and your eyes become caught in the angry stare of your older brother. He is standing there in a jacket and a tie. His girlfriend is standing next to him.

"I can't believe what I'm seeing!" he shouts. "My little sister playing on the street!" He grabs your arm.

"Let go of me!" you say, horrified and embarrassed. You are dazed. You can barely hear the words he is saying.

"Do you need money? Why didn't you ask Mom or Dad or me? How could you stand out here at night? Do you know how dangerous this is? Are you crazy?"

You cannot utter a word. Before you know it, Bobby has flagged a cab and he is handing you five dollars.

"This will get you home," he says. "Now, get going."

(continued on page 94)

You and Karen climb into the cab. You are shaking.

How could he do this to me? you think. Tears are rolling down your cheeks.

"Sixty-seventh and Madison," Bobby tells the driver, and the taxi pulls away from the curb.

"He can't rule our lives like that!" Karen says. "You are not a baby; and he is your brother, not your jailer!"

You look at Karen; you think about Bobby. Then you look out the window. The cab is two blocks from where it picked you up. Outside the window people are milling around a theater, waiting for an eight o'clock curtain. It is only seven-thirty.

"You're right!" you scream at Karen. "He can't do this to me!"

If you have the driver drop you off now, turn to page 23.

If you go home, turn to page 56.

"Okay, guys. That's enough. Here's the plan," you say. "We're all going to go horseback riding this morning . . ."

"Ha!" says Bob.

You continue. "And all hang out at the beach in the afternoon." You look at both guys.

"That sounds fair," Mark says.

"Okay," Bob agrees. "The horses are down this way."

You wander down to where the beach widens. There are ten horses lined up on the sand.

"I want a fast horse!" Bob tells the short Mexican man. The man grins and nods.

"Not me!" you say, knowing you haven't ridden in years.

Bob helps you onto the horse and you walk along the beach.

"Yahoo!" Bob yells, trotting past you. Mark is right behind him.

You kick your horse. He still walks slowly. You kick him again. No change. Bob and Mark are galloping away while you are clonking down the beach.

This is embarrassing, you think.

The boys gallop back. "Hey, come on!" Bob shouts.

"No, thanks. I like the scenery," you say.

"From a snail's point of view?" says Bob, trotting past you.

Your horse begins to follow. "Good horsie!" you say. He slows down.

(continued on page 96)

Later that afternoon you lie on the beach. Pete and Maria join you and you all play volleyball.

"Let's go have a lobster dinner," says Bob. You all agree. You are getting to like Bob. He's so strong and sure of himself . . . and filled with good ideas.

Pete, Maria, and Mark's mother take one car. You, Bob, and Mark take the other. Bob drives.

"Slow down, Bob," says Mark.

"Hey, don't worry about it!" Bob says, maintaining his sixty-five-miles-per-hour speed. "Do you see any speed limit signs?"

"Come on, Bob. You know how it is here. They never have signs!" Mark says.

"We're the Mexican express!" Bob laughs, speeding up.

Suddenly a loud-pitched noise comes from behind. Then honking.

"Oh, great!" Mark says. You turn around to see a police car waving you over.

Two policemen come to your car. "You were going too fast," one says to Bob.

"Where's a sign? What's the limit?" Bob says in a nasty tone. Mark puts his hands over his head.

"There's a sign back there," the policeman says.

"No, there wasn't!" Bob says. You begin to get nervous.

"Bob, shut up!" says Mark.

"Why? I'm right," he says.

The policemen talk to each other. Then one walks over and opens Bob's door.

(continued on page 97)

"Get out!" the man says. "You come with us!"

"I'm not going anywhere," says Bob.

"We go to the station," says the man, pulling Bob out of the car and putting handcuffs on him.

"Mark, do something," you say frantically.

"I can't," he says. "The police here do what they want. We'll follow them."

"I'm scared," you say.

"Don't worry," says Mark. "We'll get him out of this." He puts his arm around you. Suddenly you realize that Mark is really the strong one, even though Bob puts on a good act.

The cars pull into the station lot.

"Stay here," says Mark.

"No way!" you say. "I'm going with you." You take his hand, feeling secure in his grasp.

You walk into a big room full of old men, young men, women, and police. It is complete chaos.

"He goes to jail," one of the policemen says.

Bob looks at you helplessly. "But I didn't do anything!" he says.

Mark motions to Bob to be quiet and walks over to the officer. They disappear into another room. When they reappear, the officer walks over to Bob and unlocks the handcuffs.

"You can go," he says.

Quickly the three of you walk out of the station. You look at the determined, confident expression on Mark's face. You look at the defeated Bob. You all get in the car and Mark drives.

(continued on page 98)

"That cost me fifty dollars, Bob," he says. "And we were lucky at that!" He turns to you. "You all right?"

"Yeah! I'm fine," you say. "You really handled that well."

For the rest of the night Bob sulks.

As you drive home you realize that what you had thought were twin personalities are really very different. And there is no question in your mind which one you like. While Bob sulks in the backseat, you rest your head on Mark's shoulder. When you get back to the trailer, Bob goes straight to sleep. You and Mark go for a walk on the beach.

"You were wonderful," you say to Mark, squeezing his hand.

"So were you," he says, putting his arm around you. You feel warm and comfortable.

Neither of you says a word as you walk down the beach, listening to the waves, watching the reflection of the moon in the water. You are thinking that you still have another week in Los Angeles to be with Mark when he brings you close to him with both arms. He looks into your eyes and lifts your chin until your lips are touching. You feel yourself melt into his arms.

The End

"I play the guitar," you say. "And after a meal like that, I'd be delighted to provide some after-lunch music."

Craig's eyes light up. "You play? Would you really play for us?"

"That would be wonderful," Marcia says.

You go across to your apartment and bring back your guitar. You begin with a slow but dramatic piece. After the first notes you relax and enjoy the attention. Craig stares into your eyes and doesn't take the smile off his face.

"That was exquisite, my dear," says his mother. "Oh, please, play another."

You continue with other songs. When you finish playing, all three clap for you. You nod, a little embarrassed.

"That is some talent you have there, young lady," says Marcia. "Craig, you hang on to that one."

You can feel your face turning red.

Craig laughs. "That was fantastic," he says.

"Well, your meal was unbelievable!" you say. *And so are you,* you think, looking into his deep brown eyes.

"I guess we are a talented couple," he says, winking at you.

How many times can a girl blush in one day? you wonder.

"Well, I guess it's cleanup time!" he says.

"Can I help?" you ask.

"Of course not!" he says. "You are a guest in my

(continued on page 100)

house. Guests do not lift a finger. But thank you anyway."

"Well, the meal was great. Thank you for inviting me. I'm sure your dinner will be a big success," you say, feeling certain that a more sophisticated crowd would probably not object to eating brains.

"My pleasure. Remember, I'm always here if you need anything. Don't hesitate to call."

I won't! you think, smiling.

You float back to your apartment and collapse onto the couch. When Karen gets home, you tell her everything. "If you ever need anything, let me call him," you say.

"Don't worry, Miss Lovebird. I will." She laughs.

Four days go by and you see no sign of Craig. You take out the trash every day before it's even full, hoping to run into him. No luck. Every time the elevator lands on your floor, you have to fight not to rush out to see if it is Craig.

On Saturday, early in the evening, you and Karen are lounging around the house trying to decide what to cook for dinner. The phone rings.

"Hi," says a male voice. "This is Craig." Your heart drops. "Listen, I am at the Newmans' house, the ones who hired me to cater their party. They also hired a classical guitarist and he just called up and canceled. Are you busy right now?"

"Me? Busy? Uh, no," you say, flustered. Your heart begins to pound. "Why?"

"Well, I remembered how wonderfully you played

(continued on page 101)

the guitar and I mentioned something to the Newmans. They would love to have you fill in. Can you
do it?"

"Play? At the party? Uh . . ." You can't even
think. Your mind is flying in a million directions.
"Yes," you manage to utter.

"Oh, great!" he shouts into the phone, and pro-
ceeds to tell you the address. "Take a cab and we'll
reimburse you. See you soon."

You are stunned. You run into the den. "Karen,
Karen! What do I wear? What do I do? I can't
believe I just said yes!"

"Whoa. Slow down," Karen says. "What are you
talking about? Wear to what?"

You explain the phone call to Karen and she
jumps off the couch.

"Well, what are you waiting for! What are you
going to wear?" She rushes into your room. "I
know just what you'll wear," she says, taking out a
black dress with a fuchsia stripe down the side.

When you are dressed, you fling the guitar over
your shoulder, dash downstairs, and hail a cab. Before you know it, you are there.

You ring the doorbell and a tall, blond woman in a
gray-and-maroon silk dress greets you.

"You must be Craig's friend. Please come in. I
really appreciate this. I'm Catherine Newman. You
are getting me out of a tight spot. When the gen-
tleman called, I was devastated. This is a very important dinner and everything must go just right."

(continued on page 102)

Sure, you think. *Nervous? Me? Never.* You carefully concentrate on walking, afraid if you don't that your knees might give way. You smile and try to remain calm.

"I'll show you where you'll be playing and then you can say hello to Craig and get started."

"That sounds fine," you say. *How about I say hello to Craig and stay in the kitchen?* you think.

You follow Catherine into a huge living room with about twelve people scattered about. There are cheeses and pâtés on several tables and a bar at one end of the room.

You go into the kitchen. Craig is standing over a stove, stirring something. Another guy is chopping vegetables and a woman is arranging a tray filled with hors d'oeuvres.

"You made it!" Craig says, motioning for you to come over. "I can't stop stirring or this sauce will get lumps." He reaches over and hugs you with one arm. "Thanks." His wavy brown hair falls gently around his face. His warm smile makes you feel relaxed and calm.

"Are you ready?" Catherine says, popping her head into the kitchen.

"Good luck," he says.

The evening goes perfectly. During cocktails you play songs with an upbeat; and during dinner slower, softer songs. After dinner you play a combination. You are amazed at your memory. Two of the guests

(continued on page 103)

request songs, which, luckily, you know. And nearly everyone compliments you.

"Honey, you were absolutely marvelous," Catherine says when the guests are gone. "We can't thank you enough."

She hands you a fifty-dollar bill. You have never even seen a fifty-dollar bill before, let alone owned one.

"Thank you very much," you say, trying to hide your shock. You want to jump up and down and run to the phone to call Karen.

You say good-bye to the Newmans and you and Craig go outside. The night is beautiful. The air is brisk and the sky is clear.

"Catherine asked me if you and I would do another party she's having next month. I told her I would ask you," Craig says.

"I'd love to!" you say.

Craig takes your hand, squeezing it gently. "We really do make a good pair," he says softly, turning you toward him. He looks into your eyes.

You are sure you have fallen into a dream.

"I'm so glad I met you," he says.

"Me, too," you say.

He leans down and your lips meet. There is a warm tingle through your body.

If this is a dream, you think, *I hope it never ends.*

The End

You do not mention that you play the guitar. Instead, you sit for about half an hour talking to the three of them. Then the two women leave.

"I'm really glad you were able to join us," says Craig.

"You're glad?" you say. "It was incredible! I'm so impressed." *And madly in love,* you think. "I think people with talent and passion for what they do are very special."

"I agree," says Craig. "I always seem to fall for girls who have some special talent. I'm really a sucker for creative people."

Shoot, you think. *I blew it!*

The End

You arrive at the high school at 9:05 the next morning.

"Hey, Maria baby!" a blond boy yells out of a school bus window.

"Who's your friend?" another boy yells.

Maria looks at you. "See!" she says. "We'll just sit together and ignore them. Except for Pete, of course."

There are hoots and howls as you walk toward the bus.

"Here goes nothing!" Maria says, taking a step up.

You look at her, take a deep breath, and follow. The bus is filled with guys; there is not another girl in sight. And every guy is staring at you and Maria.

You are excited and nervous at the same time. And you have never seen so many good-looking guys in your life. All in one place!

"Guess what," Maria says, looking up the aisle. "We're going to have to go solo."

You look down the rows. There is at least one guy in every seat. Maria plops down next to a guy with sun-bleached dark hair.

"Hi, Pete!" she says.

Hmmm, you think. *He's cute. Maria's got good taste.*

"Hey, sit back here!" a voice yells to you from the back of the bus. "We'll show you a good time." There is raucous laughter throughout the bus.

(continued on page 106)

"No, over here. I'll teach you a few things." More laughter.

You sit down in the seat behind Maria.

"Hi, there!" says a guy with soft, scraggly blond hair. "Bob here," he says, holding out his hand. You shake it and introduce yourself.

Someone taps you on the shoulder. "Can I borrow your hair?" says a guy with dark hair and a wonderful tan sitting in the seat behind you. "Just for a moment?"

"My hair?" you say.

He reaches over the seat and picks up your long hair. "My mother taught me how to braid and I never get a chance to practice. Watch!" he says to Bob. They both laugh.

"Woooo! Mark's making his first move!" a voice yells from behind. You can feel your face becoming bright red.

Maria turns around. "Don't mind them! They're just your basic obnoxious volleyball studs. Meet Pete and Mark. Mark's the one behind you."

"Hi," you say.

"We're old friends," says Bob, putting his arm around you.

"So are we," says Mark, waving your braid in the air.

"Harmless," says Maria. "I've known Mark since I was three, when our families lived next door to each other in New York. It was through Mark that I

(continued on page 107)

met these other two nuts." She smiles at Pete. "They're quite the threesome!"

For the entire bus ride you talk to Maria and the three guys. The boys are very funny. They are such close friends that it's almost as though they have their own language.

After about forty-five minutes, the bus pulls into a big parking lot. As you file out of the bus, the coach gives you your assignment.

"Okay," he says to you and Pete. "You two will pick petals off of peony flowers." He checks his list.

"Oh, terrific," says Pete. "I love picking peony petals. That's what I do every Friday night." He turns to Bob. "What are you doing?"

"A real man's job," says Bob. "I'm gluing beet seeds on a tree trunk." Everyone laughs.

You have no idea what this is all about . . . peony petals and beet seeds? You walk inside the building with the group and you are amazed. You have never seen anything like this.

The monstrous warehouse is filled with huge floats in various stages of dress. The structures themselves are wire, papier-maché, and plaster figures and forms, sitting on what appear to be flat-bed trucks. Zillions of people are all over the place, carrying flowers, gluing things onto the forms, shouting instructions, balancing on ladders and platforms.

Maria explains that each float has a theme. The

(continued on page 108)

one you are working on is a scene from the song "Puff, the Magic Dragon." She also tells you that the outer layer of the decorations, the one that gives the float its color, must be made of something natural . . . flowers, stems, petals, seeds. And each petal or seed is individually glued on. The floats have all been designed by professionals, but the work is done by groups who contribute their wages to charity. The volleyball team is working for new equipment and uniforms.

You follow the group over to a huge structure of a dragon. There is a shaped tree on either side of the monster, and bushes surrounding him, and a giant puff of wire coming out of his mouth.

"Amazing," you say.

"Okay, guys. Get to work!" yells the coach.

"Are you ready to roll?" asks Pete, tapping your back. "Plucking peony petals. Whoopee!"

You walk to a special section where dozens of people are stripping flowers. You take one of the buckets of peonies and sit down on white butcher paper that is spread on the ground. Petal by petal, you strip each flower individually.

After a few minutes Mark and Bob appear.

"And what do you want?" asks Pete.

The two guys have terribly mischievous expressions on their faces. They burst into laughter. "We have a poem for you," says Mark.

"I don't want to hear this," Pete whispers to you.

The boys clear their throats.

(continued on page 109)

> *"Little Peter picked a pail of peony
>   petals.
> A pail of peony petals little Peter
>   picked."*

They start to laugh. At first you try to stifle your giggles, but then you give in.

> *"If little Peter picked a pail of peony
>   petals,
> where's the pail of peony petals little
>   Peter picked?"*

"I'll show you where the pail of peony petals is," says Pete, picking up the pail and chasing them. He returns in a few minutes.

After an hour and a half you are sick of looking at these big pink flowers. A tall woman comes by calling for a runner.

"I'll do it!" you shout, beating Pete to the job.

"Great," says the woman. "Follow me."

You walk along the back side of the dragon and look up at the massive form. Suddenly your eyes stop. You are looking at the most gorgeous guy you have ever seen. He is standing alone, gluing petals onto the side of the dragon's neck. He waves at you and smiles.

"Okay," the woman says. "The kids on the dragon feet need glue." She hands you a pail filled with a thick, white liquid. "The easiest way up is by the stairs on the other side."

(continued on page 110)

You pick up the glue and glance back at the cute guy. There is a ramp from the floor up to the exact place on the float where he is working.

Why not take that route? you think, wondering if it is sturdy enough to hold you.

If you go up the ramp, turn to page 74.

If you take the stairs, turn to page 115.

"We're almost there," Maria says after about fifteen minutes of driving. "This is going to be a big party. Look at all these cars!"

"I'm looking! I'm looking!" you say, amazed. The street is lined with cars for blocks. You pass by Mercedes, BMWs, Hondas, an Alfa Romeo, a Corvette. And half the cars have racks on the top for surfboards.

"These cars belong to kids our age?" you ask.

"Yes," Maria says. "You wouldn't believe the cars the kids get."

"You're right!"

"There's Lesley's house!" Maria says, pointing.

You look. There are at least one hundred people standing outside a gate and milling around the street. You can hear loud live music blaring from the house, and screaming and laughter. You cannot believe what you are seeing. New York parties are nothing like this!

Maria parks the car and you walk back to the house. You have a funny feeling in your stomach. She puts her arm around you.

"Don't be nervous," she says. "We'll have fun."

You walk past groups of people hanging out by the cars. When you get to the front gate someone yells, "How's it going, Maria?"

Maria waves back. "Hey, Tony!"

"Why are all these people out here?" you ask.

"They weren't invited, so they couldn't get in," Maria says.

(continued on page 112)

"Why would they come?" you say.

"To hang out with everyone," Maria says. You cannot imagine going to a party to stand outside.

There are two big men standing at the gate.

"They're bouncers," says Maria. "In case of trouble."

"Name," says one of the men.

Maria tells them her name.

The guy looks at his list. "Plus one," he says. "That must be you." You nod.

The other guy puts an *x* on your left hand with a bright pink marker, and you walk through the gate and around to the backyard. There is a band in the far corner and people are dancing. Others are sitting around a pool on a lower level. Most of the crowd is congregated on the patio.

Miniskirts, short dresses, tights, boots. The whole scene is overwhelming, and you suddenly feel very self-conscious.

"Maria!" says a cute guy in a V-neck sweater and jeans. He puts his arm around her.

"This is Kevin," she says. "One of the studs from school . . . and one of my best friends."

"Glad to meet you," he says.

"Me, too," you say.

Two other guys join you . . . Joe and Steve. All three are friendly, cute, and comfortable.

As you talk, you scout the mass of people, looking for Dan. *He said he would be here,* you think.

Suddenly your eyes stop. There is a guy across the

(continued on page 113)

room waving tentatively in your direction. It looks like Dan, but it's dark and you can't be sure.

"Maria, Maria," you say, nudging her. "Is that Dan?"

She looks across. "Yeah, I think so. Go over. I'll stay right here."

You take a deep breath and walk toward this guy.

"Hello!" he says, walking up to you. "I wasn't sure if it was you. I'm so glad you came. Come sit down."

You follow Dan over to a stone wall. He sits down and you sit next to him.

"So how do you like L.A.?" he asks.

"Great! I love it so far," you say. "But it is a bit overwhelming."

"But you're from New York," he says. "I didn't think anything would be overwhelming to a New Yorker."

"Well," you explain, "it's very different." And you tell him your thoughts about the two cities. As you speak, Dan looks directly into your eyes, and you have the feeling that he really cares about what you are saying.

For the next hour you and Dan talk about everything . . . school, family, friends. You are nearly oblivious to what is going on around you.

"Well, hello there," Maria interrupts. "I thought I lost you. Listen, Kevin, Steve, and Joe want to go check out another party. I'd like to go, too."

"Oh, okay," you say, disappointed.

(continued on page 114)

"Wait. You can stay if you want. We'll pick you up later," says Maria.

You look at Maria, then at Dan. Then you look around at the crowd of people, none of whom you know.

If you stay, turn to page 18.

If you go with Maria, turn to page 78.

You look at the ramp, at the glue, at the guy.

No way, you think. *I'd probably make a fool of myself.*

So you walk around the float to the stairs on the other side. You deliver the glue to the people at the dragon's feet; then you wander around looking for Maria. You finally find her gluing red petals onto the dragon's tongue.

"Hooray!" she screams. "Am I glad to see you. Let's switch jobs." She hands you a pail of red flowers. "I'm not sure how you ended up with Pete, but I'm more than willing to pick peony petals with him. See ya." She takes off.

A half hour later you finish the dragon's tongue and move over to the tree trunk where Bob and Mark are working. Seed by seed you press the tiny black balls into the glue.

This will take forever, you think, looking at the size of the float. *And it's so boring.*

Finally you finish your patch of color. You step back and look around. *It's amazing,* you think.

The dragon is exquisite . . . his skin is varying shades of green, sometimes slipping into brown. And the tree trunk is a wonderfully rich brown. All the little patches of color seem to come together in the whole. And the fiery-red tongue provides a brilliant, hot contrast.

(continued on page 116)

Every single person works on a tiny space, you think. *And in the end each individual contribution combines with all the others to create a spectacular whole.*

You are somehow overwhelmed by the idea, knowing that it describes more than just the group effort in creating a Rose Bowl float. You have always loved being involved in community projects, and you feel very excited to be a part of this one. The whole day is wonderful.

On the bus going home Mark invites you and Maria to drive to Mexico for the weekend with him, Pete, and Bob. Mark's mother and brother are staying in a house in Rosarita beach and she has told Mark that he can invite friends for the weekend.

"Will your mom let us go?" you ask Maria.

"Sure. Mark's mom is her best friend!" she says.

You have never been to a foreign country before.

"That'll be so much fun," you squeal.

By the time you get home, it is seven o'clock.

"Wow! Time sure flies when you're having fun!" says Maria. "I'm starved!"

You are famished also. Maria's mother fixes you chicken, a salad, and rice. Just as you are finishing dinner, the phone rings. Maria lets it ring twice and picks it up.

"Hello. Oh, hi, Dad . . . What?" She lets out a shriek.

(continued on page 117)

"What's the matter?" says her mother, looking worried.

"Two tickets to see Bruce Wintersteen tonight? Of course we want them! Thanks!" She hangs up and runs over to give you a hug.

"They've been sold out forever. Someone at the office does legal work for Bruce and just gave my dad two tickets for tonight's show! Come on . . . let's get ready."

You cannot believe it! You have always heard that he is incredible in concert, but it is impossible to get tickets. Now you are going!

You get dressed quickly and rush out. It's a forty-minute drive to the Coliseum. You and Maria sing all the way there. When you arrive, you pick up your tickets at the box office and hurry in.

The concert is unbelievable. He plays for three and a half hours. You have never seen anyone with such energy and vitality.

"I have to meet him! I have to!" Maria shouts when the concert ends. People start pouring out into the aisles. "Let's go backstage. Come on." She pulls you toward the front.

There is a guard standing at the entrance to the back.

Well, so much for this idea, you think.

"Follow me," says Maria.

"Sorry girls," the guard says gruffly.

(continued on page 118)

"Bruce asked us to meet him after the show," says Maria.

"Where's your backstage pass?" says the guard.

Suddenly a fight breaks out just behind you. The guard runs over. The coast is clear.

If you sneak through, turn to page 87.

If you leave, turn to page 81.

About the Author

Jan Gelman is a twenty-one-year-old senior at the University of Colorado, Boulder. She is majoring in journalism and hopes to pursue a career in photo-journalism upon graduation. *Seven-Boy Vacation* is Jan's sixth Follow Your Heart Romance; the others are *Summer in the Sun, Boys! Boys! Boys!, Faraway Loves, Take a Chance on Love,* and *Lots of Boys!*

Jan has lived both in New York City and in Los Angeles, and in writing *Seven-Boy Vacation*, she has recalled many of her own experiences and those of her friends. Like the heroine, Jan has traveled to Mexico, worked on the Rose Bowl floats, and ice-skated in Rockefeller Plaza.

Jan has a special love for travel and would like to work her way around the world, learning languages and exploring different cultures.